PREFACE

West Dreams East is the love story of Kayleigh, an Irish teacher, and Chi, a Chinese artist, set against the background of the 1989 revolutionary events in China. Chi introduces Kayleigh to Lao Yu, a Taoist nun who initiates her into Taoism, the ancient Chinese path of wisdom. When Kayleigh is deported and Chi arrested for their part in the demonstrations against the government this mystical philosophy sustains and guides them in their struggle for reunion. The book explores how the search for love and companionship is inextricably linked with the quest for truth and identity.

DEDICATIONS

This book is dedicated to my late father Joseph Hogan, the inspiring force of my travels and thirst for knowledge. It is also dedicated to my mother who nurtured my sense of adventure and my desire for freedom and learning. I would also like to thank my partner Kevin and my two children Sara and Kevin for their support and patience with me in the long journey it took to write this book. To my brothers and sisters, who helped through it all a sincere thanks. A particular mention to my younger brother Joseph who gave me the idea of applying the Chinese philosophy of Taoism to the book which was later to become a central theme. To Mary for her laughter, humorous interjections and creative ideas, to Sean for his staunchness and his smiles, to Kathleen for her praise, to Teresa for her fortitude, to Claire for her wisdom. It is also dedicated with loving memory to my godfather and uncle, Tom, who lent me a quiet room to begin the book and lots of cups of tea and laughter. To my extended family and friends too numerous to mention, but especially Patricia Houlihan and Val O"Shaughnessy who never thought any dream too wild. To Tom Moore of Janus Design for his exquisite cover and other creative support and to Deirdre Devine at Choice Publishing for her extra effort to get this book published on time. Thank you all for making my dream come true. As my father would say, thank you, thank you, thank you agus buíochas le Día.(Thank God)

AN LEABHARLANN
Coláiste na hOllscoile Corcaigh

You may write due date on Date Label
Scríobh an spriocdháta ar lipéad an dáta
FINES RIGOROUSLY IMPOSED

The Library, University College Cork

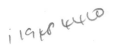

ISBN: 978-1-905451-89-0

A CIP catalogue for this book is available from the National Library.

This book was published in cooperation with
Choice Publishing & Book Services Ltd, Drogheda, Co Louth, Ireland
Tel: 041 9841551 Email: info@choicepublishing.ie
www.choicepublishing.ie

Contents:

Chapter One: In the Now.

I'll start my story in the middle where all things commence, not at the end or the inception but here in the centre of the now, the ever living present which is the only time that we really know. After all the past exists only in memory, the future is merely conjecture, the present is all we've got. Now in this moment the longing comes back to me like all intense emotion in slow motion. The longing for those early days of love's requitment when time expanded to fill the now with eternity, making it huge and significant like the stark details of a dream more real than reality itself. The air, how it smelt of almond icing, the day of the Fruit Blossom Festival when we sat under the pear tree as its delicate lemon petals drifted like confetti on the grass below. And we sang our love to each other with each gesture, word and look.

We had climbed the hill to the plateau where the blossoms were waving wedding veils in pastels pink, salmon and yellow. Chi held my hand quite recklessly; the authorities were always vigilant even on Saturdays and we didn't need to give them reason to follow our trails. The student demonstrations had just begun and there was a heady excitement in the air - a renewed sense of freedom, of hope and optimism - typical of but greater than the season of spring itself. This only served to ignite our love and fuel it even though we knew that foreigners could be used as handy scapegoats at times of political unrest, in particular when developments did not meet with Government approval. As recently as 1986 there had been expulsions of nationals from other countries who had allegedly been involved in student demonstrations that year. Their Chinese friends had also been punished for their association with them through re-education programmes, salary deductions, demotions and such like.

That day however, politics were far from our lives as we breathed in the festivity of spring love. We got off the bus at the base of the hill and swam in the tide of people in the direction of the orchards. Along the way the vendors plied their wares, everything from candied apples to ice cream, beer and hard-boiled pink eggs. Chi, preferring the personal touch, had already filled a basket from his own kitchen.

At the top of the hill was the familiar Chinese majestic gateway; four red columns supporting a massive green tiled roof overhung by a smaller one. The overall shape resembled an upside down ship. The edges were painted gold and protected by fiercesome dragons at the gables. The golden Chinese calligraphy over the central archway gloriously proclaimed the mountain's name - 'Blossom Peak.' Beyond the archways the hill levelled into a plateau of peach, lemon and white petals frolicking in the April wind. Through the trees romancing couples and groups were weaving their way to shelter under a choice arbour. Those who had found their spot were garrulously giggling their way through their spoils. The men honed in on the beer, bai jui and cigarettes whilst the women focused on the food.

We find a quiet spot under the protection of a pear tree. Like himself Chi's basket is filled with surprise. For openers he produces two exquisitely painted porcelain bowls into which he pours Chinese champagne, closer to a cider than a wine but tastes divine in the circumstances. This is followed by hand made Shanghaiese sweet dumplings; insides are sugared fruits and nuts, outside a light flour paste. Combined with the champagne the taste is tantalising. We sip and swallow through the warmth of the afternoon. As I was merrily chewing on one of the sweets my teeth hit stone hardness.

I extract it and in my hand I discover an exquisite green jade ring. I look up to meet Chi's eyes, which I find are watching me widely and lovingly.

'Well do you like, not like?' He jokingly translates the question directly from the Chinese.

'It's for me, oh my God, Chi, it gorgeous ,' I enthuse breathlessly.

'I thought you'd like the green jade - it symbolises for us Chinese eternal love. With this ring as my humble servant I wish to ask you be my partner for eternity in this life and all our lifetimes.

And with that he took the ring and slid it up my second finger, circled his arms around my shoulders and bewitched me with a heavenly kiss. My lips, my body and my soul reached in response and I felt as if our lives were entwined as one; smiled on by the Tao. (According to ancient Chinese wisdom the Tao is the source of all things, the origin before origin and the uncreatd which creates everything. Chi had introduced me to this philosophy which had provided an even stronger foundation for our union.)

Soon the practicalities started to filter through my mind. Were we to be married legally in China and if so how? Or were we to wait until I returned to Ireland after my assignment, and then would the Government give Chi permission to leave with me? Chi must have been reading my thoughts because he said.

'I've spoken to Jia, the Dean of the Arts Department about permission to arrange a wedding. He has no objections and he will speak to the other big bosses,'

'But I thought the authorities took an unsympathetic view of marriages to foreigners?'

'Normally that is so but the political climate at the moment is very liberal so *it's very* good time to move. Also I am fortunate to be in the Arts Department because they are also more open then work units in factories, for example.'

'Oh Chi, I didn't dare hope... .Set myself up for disappointment, I'm completely taken by suprise...I hadn't even entertained the possibility.'

'And now that you have had the time to entertain the idea what do you think?'

What could I say with this spectacular man close to me proposing marriage; encompassing all I had ever dreamed of in a mate; love, wisdom, humour, tenderness and scintillating sexuality? I blushed and giggled nervously despite myself but managed to say quite assuredly;

'I think it's the best idea ever imagined, I'd love to marry you, Chi.' and as I reached for him Chi's face glowed with sunlight, he swooped me up in his arms and drew me into his soul. I wanted that moment to last forever and now I know it did, in the eternity of the union with the one that is the Tao, manifest in this world in the union of opposites, of ying and yang, of male and female. Little did I know however that this was the calm in the eye of a hurricane that was sweeping over China and over our lives.

The wedding did happen shortly after that despite the demonstrations or maybe because of them since the authorities were preoccupied. It was a traditional Chinese wedding - seldom seen today except in remote areas. In Chi's hometown in the countryside we were able to procure all the necessary regalia. I was dressed completely in red; a red veil covered my head and I wore a long red silk tunic ('chi pao') embroidered in gold. I was conveyed in a red carriage on the shoulders of four bearers dressed in peasant fashion with white turbans and bare chests. A small troupe of dancing pipe players and drummers heralded my way from Chi's sister's house to the marriage chamber where Chi awaited. I can see him now at the doorway, his smile beckoning me into an eternity of bliss with him, his arm outstretched from his princely attire leading the way to the inner chamber. There under the guidance of Lao Yu, the leading light of the Mao Shan branch of Taoism, we promised eternal love to each other. She performed the traditional rituals and rites of Taoism that united us in love forever.

It is my Taoist training that lead and me to believe that Chi is still in this world today even though I haven't heard from him since his imprisonment. The meditation and mind control techniques that I learned from Lao Yu allow me to communicate on psyche levels with people of similar training, like Chi. Last night he came to me in a dream as bright as the glaring light of a North Western Chinese winter's morning. His face was round and strong, his eyes gentle and deep, he spoke in words soft and reassuring and I knew he would say he was safe. He was saying he was safe and well.

But there was pain in his face that he could not hide and I knew he was undergoing some kind of trial in prison. And before I could ask him a question his smiling pained face receded into the darkness that swallows up our dreams when our eyes open. I woke up calling his name begging him to please come back to me but I knew he couldn't for now - his powers were too weak and he had to conserve them. I descended into the depths of sadness that spawns our tears and clung to my pillow, writhing in a pitiful jelly of despair. Where are you Chi, how can I find you, how much more longing can a heart endure before it withers in the desert of deprivation?

My body exhausted my heart distraught with self-pity I reached in desperation for the succour of my Taoist training. I began to breathe the controlled, even breaths that Lao Yu's school had taught me. Slowly expanding the lungs to the point of full capacity and gently releasing the breath on the exhale. Repeating as often as needed to totally relax the body and to prepare it for the stillness of meditation. A meditation achieved by the mental recitation of a mantra or word of peace. As the other thoughts of the day congregate in the head they are gently released by the mind as it turns its attention once again towards the mantra. The eventual state achieved is more relaxed and peaceful than the deepest sleep. Western science recognises the benefits of this ancient practice, which appears to be a feature of all worldly spiritual paths, including

Christianity. Measurements done on brain waves of meditating people have shown that they attain deep relaxation with simultaneous ability to solve problems and achieve high degrees of mental alertness Thus by means of this simple method of meditation I was able to retreat into my depths, to my intuitive self, to the eye of the soul and sure enough my wisdom came to me;

'Love is the electricity of life.
Love is the energy in all things.
Love is the heart of the world.
Love is the light that guides.
Follow that light.
Do not fall behind it as you do now,
Allowing your hopes for the future
To prevent you living in the present.
Your heart has been whisked off
Into the days ahead
Into your longing for Chi.
You have lost your heart.
Bring your heart back to
Your present being.
Only then can your future materialise.
Don't go chasing your heart.
Your heart is always with you.
Your heart and Chi's heart are one under the Tao.
You are never, can never be separate.

I knew the voice was that of Lao Yu communing with my soul and with Chi's across the separation of space and time. And in the stillness of my meditation I felt my connectedness with the universe, my relation to the whole and I felt safe and harmonious once more.

I've had communication from her before, not by letter of course, any letters sent to China now are censored by the authorities. Instead she'd come to me in her meditations like she said she would, not always in a visual way like the first time. The first time I suppose she wanted to make sure I understood, knew who it was, was she. She was standing before me in the four-dimensional world of meditational vision - in a shadow play of powdered smoke and translucent light - her white Taoist tunic, her shaven head, sandalled feet, simplicity itself. Her compelling eyes revealed all the wisdom of a life spent in contemplation and service.

(She taught and practised a myriad form of the healing arts, from herbalism to energy work and her reputation preceded her. She was an advisory and confidante to all stratas of society who sought her help - very often Government officials who had an intuitive sense of the value of the Taoist guidance for governance. Her little community in the mountains was the only genuinely active Taoist monastery that was allowed to flourish in Communist China. The rest had been so severely restricted they had become mere showpieces for visitors and tourists.)

In the vision she told me she was in communication with Chi and would soon see him. Meanwhile I was to launch a petition for his release through Political Prisoners International. I have thrown myself into this work with gusto. I have a full time job with P.P.I. and I am in charge of the appeal for Chinese prisoners of conscience. We have gained a lot of support in Ireland and world-wide, thousands of signatories have been gathered and sent to the Chinese Government. We have lobbied Governments and their diplomats who show sympathy but as yet there have been no releases. Gee, look at the time, 7.30 - I'd better get up and go to the office and see if there is any good news.

Scientists nowadays propose that memory is not stored exclusively in the brain but in the genetic programme of each human cell. There must be some truth to this theory because as my feet touch the pedals of my Raleigh bike memories flow of cycling on my first Golden Phoenix bicycle among the ambling crowds of Beijing, squeezed into an easy comfort by the closeness of warm flesh rather than the hot metal blasts of fuel propelled engines. I am reminded again of my early days in China. How different I was then. Even my storytelling voice was not the same..............

Chapter Two; Foreign Friends or Foreign Devils?

Arriving at Beijing airport I can hardly believe how small and dated it is - I was expecting a Heathrow or a JFK, instead I find the 1950's airhanger atmosphere comforting and nostalgically familiar - like a soft focus scene from an old black and white movie. It's hospital-green insides are barely lit up by the occasional fluorescent bulb and the overhead fans appear to be whispering welcome in a creaking Chinese.

The crackling PA system announces the details of flights in rapid-fire Mandarin and stilted Chinglish as I follow the sweeping white robes of elegant tall Arabs to the baggage reclaim.

Here I elbow and tussle in the heaving humidity for the solitary black canvas bag that contains all my material life for the next two years.

Outside in the main vestibule I search anxiously for the placard bearing my name. 'Thank God ' I almost sigh out loud as I spot it among the many brandished by an ocean of oriental faces. I muster a cheery hello to it's bearer, the only pink face around, who I conclude to be the Programme Officer for my organisation 'Development Workers Abroad' and ask in Dr Johnson form;

' Rupert Parker I presume?'

' Quite an accurate presumption, Miss Mac Loughlin,' comes the unamused response. 'Comfortable flight I take it ?'

'Well apart from the Muslim worshippers descending into the aisles to pray prostrate towards Mecca and the unmerciful row over seats between an old Spanish couple and a pair of German hippies it was all very relaxed.'

'Nothing like an eventful trip to keep the mind active I dare say.' I notice that so far Rupert has made no attempt to meet my eyes.

'Nothing like being met at the airport at the end of it, thank you very much.'

'All in the line of duty my dear,' he continues with averted eyes. 'Let me take that rather large bag.'

'That's very kind of you.' says I, adopting his more formal tones with that chameleon tendency I have for adapting to my environment.

'Fortunately it has wheels.' I continue for the sake of conversation. 'There weren't any luggage trolleys left.'

'Never are when you need them eh?' as he turns his back with the haughty assurance of one who expects to be followed.

As I tail Rupert to the awaiting vintage-looking black sedan I notice how impeccably dressed he is, despite the steam roller heat, in cream trousers, white shirt, navy tie and blazer. Incredibly he doesn't even appear to be sweating. I begin to feel quite self-conscious of my pumping brow and soggy palms in my casual red cotton dress.

' It takes roughly two weeks for the blood cells to expand and the blood pressure to reduce in response to heat,' I console myself with the words of the pre-departure medical advisor. I remember we were also told on orientation of the Chinese preference for conservative and neat dress. (I vow to take out my more formal wear tomorrow.) Unlike the trend in Europe wealth provides no excuse for sloppiness and informality and it would be taken as something of an insult to our hosts for us to drop our standard of dress because of China's perceived poverty. This is obviously why DWA have chosen a very Oxford Don type to lead the organisation here.

I practice my 'ni hao' on the driver and get a cheeky 'hello' in reply.

I settle myself into the quaintly curtained back seat next to Rupert. Bubbling with excitement and curiosity I am propelled to question him despite the formality of his appearance and his Oxbridge manners. His grey hair is immaculately groomed as is his upturned moustache and his gold rimmed glasses encase crystal cool eyes as he sits himself stiffly upright, right hand folded over left, atop his black leather briefcase.

'I read in the orientation pack that foreigners aren't allowed drive here. Is that still the case or have the rules changed?'

'Yes the regulations are constantly changing here, but as far as I am aware foreigners are not permitted to drive anywhere in China except within the city limits of Beijing.'

'So I guess I'll make good use of my bike then.'

'That's what most of the Development Workers find. Public transport is quite reliable and efficient but generally overcrowded at peak hours.'

'Like in those photos of people hanging out the back and sides and windows of buses.'

'Well, that's against the law though like most things illegal anywhere it still occurs.' Rupert delivers this information with his hands still folded and his eyes not meeting mine. 'Sardines in a can would be quite euphemistic indeed'.

'Seems like a bike is your only woman.' I break a laugh to conceal my discomfort at his distancing, impersonal tone. Rupert continues undistracted by me;

'Indeed. The bicycle lanes and the lack of motorised vehicles render one pretty safe.'

'Oh is that because individual Chinese aren't allowed to drive private cars either.'

'That's correct, only the work unit or 'dan wei ' is allotted a car with a driver, to be used by the leaders for official functions.'

'We'll probably have to introduce a similar system in the west with the gridlock and pollution problems we are experiencing.'

'Too true, too true. China definitely could not sustain the number of cars per head that the Europeans and Americans have, what with the current pollution and overcrowding problems.'

'Yes, I read that pollution and overpopulation are the major developmental concerns of the Government because the basic needs of the people have already been met.'

'Yes indeed, but I'd prefer if I may to discuss those issues with you another time.' Rupert clears his throat with a gufty guffaw and I notice his face and voice take on an even more solemn dimension. Even still he doesn't look at me but straight ahead at some unknown destination as he continues;

' I know you attended the orientation course in London and you seem to have done your reading but as you missed the in-country briefing I feel obliged to summarise the main point. The number one thing to remember is that although China has now become more open to foreigners than probably any time in it's previous history this does not mean that the Government is open to everything we foreigners have to offer.'

His face is intent, his voice earnest, his hands sway in lecturing mode.

'The English Language programme of which you are a part is a particularly sensitive area. The authorities are well aware of the need for an international language of communication but this does not mean that they wish the general population to adopt the politics, culture, or mores of the society from which this language emanates. It is one thing to teach the language it is another to promote western-style politics, religions, values or fashions.'

'But surely it is difficult to separate these issues, after all language is an integral aspect of culture.' I try to sound intelligent despite my confusion.

'That's true and we had a lot of discussion about this but the consensus seems to be that we are not seen to be proselytising religion, politics or western values. For example two American teachers were recently deported for having Bible studies in their home. And two of our female development workers were asked to dress more respectfully in class.'

'Well, Bible studies wouldn't be my speciality but I'm curious to know what the girls were wearing?

'Well in one instance a class of male students complained that they couldn't concentrate on their studies because the teacher was wearing a mini-skirt.'

'My God, this sure isn't California is it? (We had been warned about the puritan influence of communism) ' Now I am intrigued to know what happened in the other case.'

'Oh, not quite as dramatic, the teacher was wearing sandals'

'You mean you can't wear sandals in class, even in summer?'

'It was the particular type, the Chinese considered them too similar to the plastic tongs they wear around the house.'

'Now that one I would have missed but as for openly advocating western styles or values they needn't worry about me in that respect. I'm not that impressed with our western ways.'

'Nevertheless you do need to be aware before you present any materials in class of their suitability or otherwise and be sensitive in the way you express your opinions.'

'Is it true that our classes will have class monitors to keep an eye on these things.'

'Yes and that's true for the Chinese as well as for the foreigners. It is a way to keep everyone in line. In most cases you won't even know who the class monitor is.'

'But don't they all report to the communist party representative for the college?

'Yes but in secret.'

'Sounds like a spy network.'

'That's how some people interpret it but there is no need to get too paranoid'. 'The system is a lot more relaxed these days than it used to be. Just use your common-sense and avoid provocation.'

'What about the Foreign Affairs Office or 'Wei Ban' will they be keeping an eye on us too.'

'In general they are there to assist you in the practicalities of settling in and adjusting. They will assign you a Chinese teacher, an apartment and help organise your travel tickets. But you must also be aware that they are there to ensure that you abide by the regulations. So it is as well to keep them happy.'

'Sounds like we'll have a lot of people to keep happy besides ourselves.'

'Yes you are entering a highly structured, political society.'

'Do they really enforce all the rules - like applying for official permission to stay in a Chinese person's house?'

'As in any system it depends on the individuals and in China that can often depend on distance from the central Government. It some cases this renders a province more conservative but in most cases not. Your area is quite liberal from what the previous Development Workers said. But just remember DWA is a development organisation and as such is non-political so if you do decide to become politically active we will release you from your contract.

'Oh........well, that was made pretty clear by DWA from the start. Anyway it seems like the Chinese authorities will be the first to press the eject button'.

'Indeed.' responds Rupert with predictable formality.

Although I don't agree with DWA's non political stance as they call it I can see for practical reasons why they adopt it. They are here by the leave of the Chinese Government and therefore have to agree to their conditions. But to say that they are apolitical or non political is a bit of a joke because really they are conforming with the politics of the Chinese Government. This was made pretty clear in the case of a DWA teacher in Tibet who got no support from DWA when she complained of discrimination towards the Tibetan students. She was subsequently released from her contract and no new teachers are now assigned there. Politics is not my baby but I do find injustice difficult to bear. I hope I'm not put to the test in that area as I can be quiet passionate. As for the spy-ring it all seems a bit unreal if not intriguing. Probably flavoured by a dose of western paranoia too. Imagining ourselves so important in the Chinese scheme of things to be spied on.

To lighten the atmosphere (some hope) after the lecture I remark;

'The airport seems quite a distance from the city.'

'Yes, about thirty kilometres, so you are fortunate not to be subjected to my driving.'

'I'll thank communism for that so. It's nice to get a chance to see the countryside around Beijing in summer, it's very pretty.'

I peer out past the faded lace curtains at the flat fertile land beyond the tree-lined road. The fruit and vegetable fields are divided by irrigation canals and every now and then the odd androgynous human appears bent over busily in peaked straw hat and blue/grey Mao suit. The fiery sun begins to wane to a peach evening glow.

'I don't suppose there are any food shortages in Beijing - the market gardening looks very intensive and productive here.' My curiosity draws Rupert in again.

'Since the relaxation of state control of the economy and the introduction of the capitalist system food supply has been abundant. Fresh fruit, vegetables, meat are all available daily at the so-called 'free markets' in Beijing. There may not be quite the same variety in the provinces but there are few shortages of staples.'

Although he's formal and aloof I must admit Rupert's a library of information so I continue the inquisition;

'But is it true that the introduction of free enterprise has led to rampant inflation and that many people can't afford to buy food?'

'In the beginning yes, inflation rocketed to thirty per cent or more but since then there has been government intervention to control it. Still it is a problem especially for those in state employment like civil servants, doctors, and teachers. Their salaries have remained stagnant while prices rise. Farmers and entrepreneurs on the other hand are beginning to make what in Chinese terms are small fortunes. Government support to education and the social services is being reduced in Thatcherite fashion and this is causing discontent among the students and intellectuals.'

'So the social services will have to become profit-making? Isn't that a bit much to expect from a system that has been Government funded for so long?'

'That's what the intellectuals, students and civil servants think so I suppose there will have to be some compromise or else the Government may be facing demonstrations similar to those in 1987.'

'It's unlikely that it will come to that though, isn't it?'

'It's hard to tell. There is a real feeling of openness in China today; political and social issues that were never previously publicly mentioned are now being discussed everywhere, in the classroom, on the street and at meetings. Despite what the party leaders maintain the economic liberalisation has lead to a liberalisation in political views and their expression.'

'We are really privileged to be here at such an exciting time in China's history, considering that a few years back there weren't any foreigners here at all'

'Indeed - this is definitely a turning point. It will be interesting to see what the people and the Government make of it.'

The conversation wanes. Suddenly a man on what looks like a lawnmower darts across our path forcing the driver to break to a screeching halt. We are flung forward, heads butting the front seats. Stunned, I search Rupert's face for consolation but find him as inexpressive as ever. he merely adjusts his tie and regains his seat. The driver looks unperturbed and casually restarts the engine.

'Oh my God,' I gasp, 'he didn't even turn his head.'

'Oh happens frequently - most people have no idea of the rules of the road.'

'But what was that vehicle he was driving - it looked no bigger than a lawnmower?.'

'It's a product of Chinese intermediate technology, a tiny tractor with an engine the size of a motorbike, developed for smaller size farms.'

'I suppose it would be impossible to drive a European model through the paddy fields.'

'Which is why these are so popular here and in other developing countries; cheap, versatile and light weight. The Chinese today are the master inventors of intermediate technology - as they were in the past.

'But watch out for the Kamikaze drivers!'

'And there are a lot of them out there.'

'So far the traffic is surprisingly free-flowing.'

'This is considered the best constructed and least congested highway in China, though in general traffic flow is good in Beijing. The main problem is the unpredictability of the people - jaywalking is quite common, and I have often seen traffic going completely the wrong way around roundabouts. But the truck drivers are a law unto themselves- still believing might is right they rarely concede to bikes or pedestrians.'

'So how do people get across the road?'

'At junctions cyclists and pedestrians cluster together and cross en masse.'

'Well that will take getting used to. Oh! this must be the suburbs of Beijing.' and I feel the curiosity swell in my veins only to be dampened by Rupert's remark;

'Yes they go on endlessly uniform and grey.'

To my eyes however it looks a lot more modern then I expected; high-rise apartment buildings and eight-lane free ways. Apart from the massive bicycle lanes and the low density of the traffic it could be anywhere in the world.

Rupert persists in giving the conservationist lecture in good old Prince Charles mode -he must have had private tuition.

'When Mao took over the city in1949 his aim was to modernise the 'primitive' Imperial capital. He did so by destroying much of old Beijing, over eight thousand temples and monuments and even the walls and gates of the city. In it's place he built a Soviet-style planned city with high-rise buildings, ring roads and avenues.'

'Fortunately he retained the Forbidden City and the Temple of Heaven.' I point out - not wanting him to get too carried away.

'Yes, the Forbidden City is still considered the core of Beijing. And the Temple of Heaven is a marvel of Ming dynasty architecture,' he admits. 'But it's in the remaining old narrow alleyways or 'hutongs' that connect the main streets, with their markets and stalls, that the heart of the city resides, in my opinion.'

'Can't wait to check it out and go for it as the Americans say.'

'We haven't far to go now - the college is in the North Western part of the city, close to the airport, which is very convenient.'

As we meander down the boulevard along with other Eastern European style vehicles, sandwiched between the throngs of sauntering cyclists, my heart appears to adopt a different beat. It slows down to the ambling rhythm of the bicycles; the predominant city pulse. And I begin to wonder at the audacity of us Westerners to think that we are the centre of the world when more than half the world's population resides here in the east. And I begin to see why the Chinese consider their country 'Zhong Guo' to be 'the central kingdom.' Though I suppose that's as ethnocentric as us Westerners - all of us humans seem to suffer from the same disease of self-centredness.

The driver slows down as we approach the entrance of a large modern, grey four-storey building complex. The entrance itself is the most notable architectural feature - a large stone archway flanked by giant red dragons bearing the name of the college in golden calligraphy-'Beijing College of

Languages.' The grounds are compact with a volleyball pitch on the right and a car park and larger bicycle park to the left.

I am escorted up two flights of stairs to a modest bedroom painted the same hospital green as the airport interior - that paint must be on prescription. What can I say except that familiarity breeds a certain type of comfort.

I thank Rupert at the doorstep and agree to meet downstairs with the rest of the Development Workers for supper. My first real Chinese meal - I can't wait. And meeting all the others again - a chance to catch up on things and share impressions. I've arrived a week later than the rest for this language training in Beijing as I got special leave for my sister's wedding. I've studied Chinese in evening classes at Trinity College Dublin so I hope not to be too far behind. My thoughts exhaust me and I collapse on the single bed until I am woken by gentle tapping on the door.

'Kayleigh, Kayleigh, it's Molly. Are you awake?'

'Yes, I think so. Just a minute.' After a few seconds of disorientated daze I realise I have woken up in China, my God I am in China at last, at the Beijing School of Languages and that's Molly at the door. My eyes are dazzled by the daylight blaring through the single blue curtain and the hospital green walls. I struggle with the rusty lock and soon we are hugging each other.

We became fast friends on the pre-departure training courses in Bristol and there's an added reassuring intensity to seeing a familiar face in a foreign land.

We huddle together on the bed and exchange gossip about the wedding and the Chinese language training.

'Well, was there any craic or fights at the wedding? asks Molly spoiling for fun as usual.

'No fights, thank heavens, my mother would have had a weakness what with all the worry on the day. Oh God, the fuss, it was enough to drive anyone demented. The hardest thing was to get the bridesmaids to agree on the dresses; that was the closest anyone came to a fight. In the end they agreed

to an unusually modest and becoming beige. All there was left
to fuss about then was that everything matched from the
serviettes to the flowers to the toilet paper. God protect me
from an Irish wedding.'

'Which is the real reason you are hiding out in China - well
did he show up?'

'Of course he did as charming as any rogue, trying to
convince me that he had been all wrong in leaving me and
that he would take a slow train to China to get me back. He's
threatening to come and visit me once I get settled and to
bombard me with love letters in the meantime.'

'Well do you think you'll be able to resist?'

'I know my weaknesses that's why I'm here away from his
manipulations and power trips.'

'Nothing like distance to dampen the coals.'

'That's what I'm hoping anyway' I return queasily.

Molly puts her hand on my knee and consoles, 'don't worry
you are strong and he's miles away.'

'You're right', I respond and cheerfully I ask to change the
mood, 'Do you want to hear one of the jokes?'

'Oh, you are awful but I like you, go on'

'It's not even a dirty one....this lad was coming home from
school one day and he found a grenade on the road'

'As is commonly the case in rural Ireland'

'Suspend disbelief if you may, the point being he didn't
know what it was - it being such an uncommon find. So he
took it home to his mother who knew that it was live, whipped
it out of his hand and threw it over the back wall. Where did it
land but in the outside toilet where the old man was busily
engaged in doing his business. The grenade exploded and the
old man fled with his trousers down shouting,

' Jesus, woman what did you give me to eat?'

'Not bad...could be better. What about a bar of a song after
that.'

'What about some liquid refreshment first?'

'Give us the song first and you'll get the liquid refreshment if it's deserved'

'This is one from Uncle Jack's repertoire about the intruder in her Majesty's palace'

'How does it go?' and Molly's eyes gleam in anticipation.

'Well you'd have to have a few pints on you and a big burly Irishman with his shirt tails out and a straight face to deliver it'

'Ah come on don't be teasing me give us an ole bar'

'OK, just imagine I'm sucking on a microphone, with a pint in one hand and it goes like this;

Chorus.

'Over the wall, over the wall, the randy ole whore he jumped over the wall

All the coppers in England were no use at all

When the randy ole whore he jumped over the wall'

1

'He got to her room when the night it was dead

Saw the black negligee on the four poster bed

'Have a whiskey,' says she, 'I don't mind at all.'

'Thank God,' says the ole Queen,' you jumped over the wall'

'That's all I remember.. I suppose it's just as well'

'Yeah, says Molly, not very politically correct - aren't DWA supported by one of the Royals'

'Don't worry - you can trust an Irish person to stay out of politics or religion,' I joke.

Molly guffaws and then turns to me in uncharacteristically serious tone,

'How do your poor parents feel about you being in a communist country - mine have turned to their rosary beads?'

'Oh sure they think I am a modern day missionary who will show the way by my good example. Their only worry is that I won't find a Church to preach in'

'And how do you see yourself?'

'I'm just here to help through the English language programme. And I'm open to learning whatever I can from this ancient culture.'

'Me too', her face full of enthusiasm, 'I was reading up on Taoism, the oldest indigenous philosophy. Fascinating stuff - full of seemingly contradictory statements like your weakness is your strength. The Taoist believe in the union of opposites, of ying and yang, positive and negative and their thinking is different from our western logic that holds that you cannot propose the truth of two contradictory statements.'

'Yeah, I studied Taoist philosophy in the States and I found it intriguing too. I hear there are still some active Taoist monasteries left. I'd love to visit some of them.'

'Em,' says Molly and she leans back on the bed and rolls her eyes in the direction of the ceiling, 'imagine a Yul Brenner look- alike monk, not celibate of course, guiding you along the pathway of enlightenment.'

'I can see him now,' as I lay down on the bed beside her and nudge her off, ' taking the pathway to the haybarn'

'Hey I was just getting comfortable,' says Molly as she picks herself up from the floor.

'Just a little bit too comfortable and carried away; besides you've told me nothing about the language course'

Molly joins me sitting up on the bed again and says in that conspiratorial way that some women have of divulging information:

'Already there's stiff competition as to who's the most proficient in Chinese. Both Rupert and the Chinese teachers are pushing us hard to study. We have classes all day and we're supposed to do homework in the evenings. Not much time for extra-curricular activity,' she moans.

'Why all the pressure?'

'Well, it's the first language training course specifically geared for foreign teachers of English in Beijing so the College are anxious that it is successful. And of course Rupert doesn't want to waste DWA funds. Plus it's getting a lot of outside attention.'

And she begins to point her fingers in teacherly fashion to illustrate.

' The Department of Education is holding a banquet in our honour, we'll be on the National News, they are going to do a documentary on us for TV and we will also be interviewed by the newspapers.'

'Gee, we're going to be stars and none of our friends and family will be here to witness it. You have to go to a foreign land to be appreciated.' I chuckle and so does Molly.

'You think that's funny - well, one of our group assignments is to write a song in Chinese and the best groups get to sing it for the cameras.'

'That sounds a bit ambitious - the Chinavision song contest - hilarious.' We giggle.

'No the most hilarious thing is that this Scottish guy, called Robby 'ach aye' Mac Donald, who no one can understand in English, has been dubbed the best student already, by the Chinese teachers.

'Must be something to do with the sing-song of the Scots accent.'

'Yeah, that's supposed to give us Irish an advantage too but this guy's a real swot.'

'Or else he's trying to impress a cute Chinese teacher.'

'More likely the latter but more power to him - oh there's the dinner bell'

And we do a mock highland fling out the door.

'I'd better warn you,' says Molly as we negotiate the concrete stairs, 'there's a few of the lads who don't seem to have the Development Worker spirit. In other words they are a bit gluttonous with the food. You know the way all the food is served clockwise from a revolving inner table - well these guys plonk themselves at the top of the table and take huge helpings before spinning the food on to the rest. So there's very little left for anyone else. Of course none of the girls have said anything yet coz they're Western lads and they'll be pretty thin on the ground after this week. Most of them are already prejudiced against forming relations with Chinese guys for various reasons, social, cultural, political and even physical (something about size - ahem.) Anyways, instead of saying anything they just avoid their tables at mealtimes.'

'So why haven't you said anything if you 're so disinterested in their bodies?'

'Back-up, my dear, back-up. But now that you are here I think it's time to pounce.'

'Don't worry I'll be a firm ally, sister.'

In the lounge we notice there has already been a rush on the tables without the culprit guys and we are forced to join the barbarian eaters. The bold-faced nature of their scoffing of our dishes by contrast to the delicate placing of each dish by the self-effacing Chinese waitress is enough to make anyone puke- except there's no food to puke on. I glare at them, impatient for Molly's chastisement.

'Nobody said anything,' she addresses herself at last at the threesome, 'in the first few days because we wanted to give you lot the benefit of the doubt. I mean we thought you may not have done your homework on Chinese eating customs, or you were suffering from shell shock from the flight but it's apparent now that neither of these feature in your disgraceful behaviour. Since logic, common-sense, decency or courtesy appear never to have graced your paths you leave me no option but to state the case plainly. Those at the top of the table are to take an individual portion from each dish which then has to be circulated to other members at the table so that each may receive an individual portion. In this way everyone gets some of each communal dish to eat. Do you get my drift or would you prefer a Chinese translation?

There's a stunned silence from the lads never guessing that their might would be questioned. It takes time before the leader speaks.

'If you know so much about Chinese customs why don't you give us a lecture on it sometime when we have time to listen. Right now we would just like to finish our meal.'

'So would we,' I thunder back at him for all to hear, 'except the difference is we don't have any food to finish. Now either you take individual size portions like decent human beings or we swing the table anti-clockwise.'

By this time the whole of the room is listening and the older Development Workers already aware of our plight clap and herald support. 'Here, here!' they shout in unison, 'about time you boys got manners.'

The trio bang their dishes and cutlery down as they leave the table wine-faced.

It was the most delicious meal myself and Molly had ever eaten and we languished over and savoured each victorious bite. Later we celebrated in the common room with Chinese beer or 'pi jui ' which in our triumphant state tasted like champagne despite the unhappy approximation of it's sound in English. (Ex-pats jokingly refer to it as 'piss juice.') It was little battles like this, won in the early days, that prepared and sustained me for the tougher ones yet to come.

Just as we Westerners have traditionally worshipped the sun the Chinese revere the moon which they regard as the representation of the feminine principle in nature. Chinese astronomers have studied the moon in detail in all it's phases, throughout the ages. The Chinese calendar is a lunar one, and although the solar calendar of the West has been in official use since 1911, the lunar calendar is still observed for fixing dates of festivals and birthdays. Many Chinese are unable to give their age in Western years. A lunar month is the interval between new moons 29 or 30 days. Years of 12 moons (354 or 355 days) and 13 moons (383 or 384 days) are interspersed to make the long term average of 365.24 days. Chinese music and song radiate with reference to the moon and it's connection to affairs of the heart. The Chinese believe that when you look at the moon you are united with family, friends and loved ones no matter where they may be.

On my first night in China a full moon bathes my bedroom in a milky light and sends me in my dreams back to Ireland. I relive more vividly than the initial experience my sister's wedding; the brilliant colours, the lilting voices, the sprightly music wrapping me in a whirlwind of sensual delight. Here she is; gliding down the aisle a resplendent Grecian Goddess in her bridal dress, the groom basking in her beauty, she glowing with his love. Awe-struck compliments are hushed from the congregation. Together they recite for my ears alone, Shakespeare's quintessential sonnet to true love;

'Let me not to the marriage of true minds admit impediments
Love is not love which alters when it alteration finds
Or bends with the remover to remove
Oh, no it is an ever fixed mark
That looks on tempests and is not shaken.'

'Oh no! not him again - why did they have to invite him to the wedding - here he is - his face is breathing into mine - his smile making a mockery of my tears - his callous blue eyes sucking all my life-force into them - his hands are on me and I wake up with the sensation of insects crawling all over my skin. I grope frantically for the light.

My scream must have woken the whole corridor, but I don't hear a sound except the scampering across my bed of a zillion cockroaches onto the bedside table. I can hardly breathe. I jump out of bed in a cold sweat shaking until I can calm down. Did he bring on the cockroaches or the cockroaches him?.

Why is the past always sneaking up on the present? I thought I'd forgotten the anguish of love's first betrayal. The pain of being two-timed and being one of the last to know. Of he parading into class with the girl he had exchanged as casually as a new coat for me. The humiliation in front of a close-knit class of Second Year Literature. How translucent my body felt. As if everyone was peering into my soul and watching it rupture. The long months of waking every morning worn away with tears. Egging myself to get up and face the day, face college, face my friends and colleagues and ultimately face 'them' as they flaunted their new found love in class after dreary class, hour after hateful hour.

Then suddenly one day as if by some miracle of insight she became a mirror of me and the two of them a mirror of us until finally we became the farcical fools of a Shakespearean Comedy. Clinging, cloying, dependent lovers who know nothing of the mature, independent, boundless love of the sonnet.

And this parody of love becomes just a lesson to me of the many disguises false emotion takes. By knowing loves ridicule we learn to know the real thing. So I reject again this hypocrisy and stamp it from my life just as I begin to do to these cockroaches clambering for shelter in the light. When I am sure that everyone of them is dead and swept from the bed and table I settle back in for a more restful sleep.

At seven o'clock my ears are shattered by the peal of the college PA. Chinese folk music is blaring throughout the college. Even the ear plugs I remembered to bring provide no protection against the crackling clamour. This PA system was adopted by the party during the Cultural Revolution as a means of propagating the prevailing ideology. It remains on in work units and public places today as a vindictive way of getting people out of bed, of initiating morning exercise, making announcements, delivering news and as a supposed mode of entertainment. It's the most torturous form of noise pollution I have ever come across - but ' Oh Ye and Up She Rises Early in the Morning.'

I join the others in the communal shower amidst conversations about the latest stomach affliction to have hit the group.

'Diarrhoea or constipation, you'll only get one if you're lucky so take your pick. More usually it swings from one to the other,' announces my cheerful neighbour Rose. 'Or you could be really fortunate and get dysentery and lots of concern like Joan.'

'Dysentery, that's really serious isn't it?' and a hear my voice go shrill.

'Never mind her,' says Paula, 'we're not sure that's a proper diagnosis. Besides if you follow the guidelines, eat sensibly and make sure the hygiene's good where you eat, you shouldn't have any problems.'

'That sounds more optimistic I reply.'

'Even if you do get sick, says Rose, 'you've always got the adventure of exploring Chinese traditional medicine. One of the girls got a box of tiny glass bottles filled with potions and minuscule pills to take. She's calling it the great taste sensation.'

The breakfast food isn't nearly as exciting as the dinner. The tea is pea-coloured and watery and the rice soup tastes like flour in brine. I never really get to grips with Chinese breakfast. Steamed bread being the best of it. Neither noodle soup or the soggy fried bread ever appeal to me.

Class starts at 8 o' clock and already it's quite advanced. They are using the characters to write everything down and I'm only familiar with pinyin, a phonetic alphabet adopted to translate Chinese sounds into the closest English equivalent. I write down the approximate sound for what I can hear. But the young female teacher soon realises I am slacking because there are only eight students to concentrate on. During the break she eagerly suggests that she gives me extra hours in the evening so I can catch up. Her enthusiasm is infectious so I muster a hearty reply;.

'Of course, I would, that's really kind of you,' though I had hoped to do some sight-seeing that evening with Kay.

At lunch I meet up with my future colleague at the Lanyuan Teachers College, Julie Howard from Brighton.

She's cheerful and alert and we seem to share similar views about teaching, China and recreation.

'I've heard that our college is a bit anxious that they've got two single girls again this year she tells me because last year the female teachers went back to England with two of the brightest teachers, one from our college and the other from the Medical College.

'We'll have to pick the dumber ones this year then,' I chuckle.

'Well they're not running a risk with me .... I have a boyfriend who will be visiting during the summer holidays.'

'Oh, that means the Foreign Affairs Officer will be homing in on me then.'

'Not only the 'Wai Ban,' seemingly all male and female relations are watched with intensity by everyone. The communists are supposed to be very puritanical about sex. It's frowned upon to be seen on your own with a man unless you have an approved relationship with him and the work unit must give their consent to all marriages.

'Must be part of the population control policy, I suppose. But there must be deviations - like in all societies.'

'Well, you can put it to the test if you like - I'll do the observing.'

'No way. I came to China to get away from men not to attract them.'

'That's what we all say.'

Most Chinese go for a siesta in the middle of the day to compensate for the early rising hour I suppose. I believe in acquiring the customs of one's adopted country, in particular when they accord with one's own natural inclinations. I still feel quite jet-lagged and if it wasn't for Molly calling in on me I might have missed out on another heavy Chinese language session. Some relief from the monotony of rote learning is introduced in the late afternoon when we are given our group assignment for the song contest.

We decide on the melody from 'My Bonnie Lies Over the Ocean', as none of us are musicians and all of us know this one. The words are another thing. Susan, a middle-aged journalist from Norfolk, suggests we concentrate on one theme. I jokingly propose food since it appears to be a dominant feature of Chinese life. The others agree it's a good start and Brian an agriculturist suggests we extend it to our appreciation of all things Chinese.

'In the line of we're very happy to be in China and in this college, says Daniel, a retired teacher and wartime radar operator from Bournemouth.

OK, adds Barbara, the group leader, 'lets' try to get some words up on the board in Chinese.'

We come up with the following ingratiating verse, among others;

'We're very happy to be in China
We're happy to learn Chinese
We love the Chinese customs
Especially the Chinese cuisine'

The Chorus goes on to eulogise over a Beijing speciality, dumplings.

'Beijing dumplings, oh, they taste delicious!
Beijing dumplings oh, they are the best!'

Believe me it does sound more sophisticated in Chinese but what you are not going to believe is that we win the first prize. You guessed it the competition was pretty weak. Here I am with a group of fellow 'feeling awkward' foreigners, singing a Chinese song to the melody of a Scots ballad for Chinese national TV and it doesn't really seem that strange. Must be settling in after all. The week has just flown past and I flop into bed every night.

I manage to steer through the streets of Beijing on a bike

without damaging myself or any one else, despite the crock that is my lot. Most of the bikes available in China would have been sent to bicycle heaven in Ireland by now. The only thing that works on them is the quaint Chinese trade mark, 'Golden Dragon.' All remaining parts have to be submitted to the roadside bicycle repair for the once over, otherwise they would be surgical instruments. My brakes are gone, the ball bearings are worn, the pedals are loose to mention but a few minor complications. It is a big heavy cumbersome black bike of the kind my grandfather would have had but amazingly the Chinese are starting to export them West. Stephen Roche, the Irish champion cyclist got a gift of one from the Chinese Government.

But despite the hazards or maybe partly because of the hazards cycling in Beijing is fun. There's just so much activity and on your bike you have the opportunity to observe at leisure. The Chinese are a nation of neck-strainers and any action on the street is theirs to behold. Despite what we were told in our 'cultural orientation', that it's considered 'loss of face' to lose one's temper in public we find exceptions to this cultural rule early on.

We were also told in our briefing on culture that there is no word in the Chinese language for privacy and privacy as we Westerners understand it does not exist here. This it seems is in part due to the population density particularly in big cities, where large extended families often share only two rooms, in part due to the influence of communism which stresses the communal rather than the individual side of people and also due to the predominant peasant culture (80%) which emphasises, in Confucian fashion, family duty and obligation over personal rights.

Molly and I experience one aspect of this when we stop to look at a map on the roadside. Immediately the map is whisked off us from behind and we turn around to find the culprit, a wide-smiling youth, is not interested in showing us the way but in seeing what we've got. He takes a good look at it and pointing at something familiar to his friend he offers it back without so much as a courtesy. We're too open-mouthed to say anything but we hear similar stories from the rest of the crew.

Along the roadside too we find all kinds of peddlers and trades people; noodles, kebabs, sweets, fruit, vegetables, toys, arts and crafts sellers alongside keymakers and bicycle and shoe repairers. The unfolding of this colourful drama of life together with the intimacy of rubbing elbows with so many easy-going strangers adds to the delight of the ride. If you were to do nothing but cycle around Beijing all day you could never possibly get bored or road fatigued which begs the question of the advancement that has really been brought by the proliferation of the great automobile in the West.

Our last night as a group in Beijing is to be marked by a Chinese banquet given in our honour by the Department of Education. And what a feast it is! Some of it is to go out live in National TV so we have to be on our best behaviour. We joke with the reformed gluttons about this and time having eased the tension we steal a smile. There are about sixty people in the large dining hall seated around round tables; thirty development workers interspersed with Chinese Government representatives and teachers. Customary toasts and speeches are made but we've been warned not to drink much of the 'evaporate while you wait' 'bai jui', the white rice alcohol. Obviously some of the Chinese officials thought they needed some to help along their speeches and Molly and I smile knowingly across at each other as the guy next to her sways from side to side.

The dishes are plied lavishly by waitresses dressed in silken red 'qi paos', the traditional tunic, with daring modern slits up to the knee and beyond. Both of my neighbours are Chinese 'Cadres' or Government officials who don't speak English and though I barrage them with questions about what we are eating I'm not always sure that I understand the answers. What I originally thought was beef now appears to

be dog meat. To confirm my worst expectation I put my fingers on my head in imitation of horns and say in Chinese,
'Did this meat come from this,' and the response is
'No, it came from....'.and my neighbour imitates a dog's growl. Well no point in regretting after all I have already eaten most of it and it tastes as succulent as beef to me. And of course I do not want to offend my hosts who consider dog a great delicacy. Moreover if you eat meat anyway how can you really start to draw distinctions between what animal it comes from.

Nevertheless, I decide to question my hosts more thoroughly before I eat anything else. The frogs legs take a while to identify. I thought they were an exotic bird's limbs as they were heavily disguised in a rich batter. But my neighbour tells me they belong not to a bird but a little animal and when he makes hopping movements with his hands across the table it finally twigs with me. He laughs out loud when he sees my reaction, but I had to admit it is exquisite despite my prejudices. Soon I begin to loose track of what I am eating as one exotic dish follows another; Chinese radishes in white, lemon and rugby reds; some mushrooms the size of plates and others the texture and colour of wood; greens of subtle shades and varying fibre; and fish, fowl and flesh served in a multitude of forms and decoration, in dumplings, in batter, in sauces, in syrups with nuts, with fruit and vegetables.

The only dish I take exception to is of course one of the greatest delicacies of Chinese Cuisine; 'Sea Cucumber' as it is euphemistically called, but the more appropriate and deserving translation would be 'Sea Slug.'

My cuisine guide informs me that it is a creature that cannot be classified as plant or animal that lives at the bottom of the sea and because of it's rarity it is highly prized. I wonder at the sense of this as I try to shove a piece of this slimy, primeval, dank glob into my mouth and force a smile and appreciation to the eagerly awaiting Chinese hosts.

'Ah, wei dao hao gei le ' 'It tastes very delicious,' and I tell my first white lie of many in Chinese. Lack of appreciation for one's host's food constitutes severe
'loss of face ' both for the guest and the host. There is no exact equivalent in English or this cultural concept which embraces a series of complicated rules governing behaviour in the East. The closest translation would be to cause embarrassment to oneself or another or to let the side or oneself down. Mastery of this and other cultural mores will be very important to my integration into Chinese society and in the success of my work as a teacher. I see this as an exciting challenge.

But to continue with the feast - colour and presentation are obviously as important as texture and taste. One dish in particular takes our eyes away, a large phoenix carved out of vegetable marrows, radishes, carrots and fruits I don't recognise, positioned as a centrepiece for the meal.

The highlight (in this case the most startling event of the outing) like all such moments was kept until last. From the kitchen emerges a retinue of waitresses carrying in pairs on a silver platter atop a bed of brightly coloured citrus fruit what looks like an enormous mechanical golden fish. The head of each fish is moving slowly left to right and it's river eyes sink into mine when it catches me gaping. Each fish is dutifully placed on the revolving table as the foreigners look frantically across at each other, not knowing where else to look.

Then arises the hum of nervous foreigners beseeching their Chinese host as to the nature of this creature, animal or manmade. The universal response is that it is a golden carp, a symbol of good luck in China. These fish are boiled with the head delicately secured out of water so that the nervous response in the head remains although the fish is technically dead. It required great skill and patience as well as access to a fresh supply to accomplish the marvel we as honoured guests are now beholding. My slightly tipsy Chinese neighbour takes great delight in adding to the spectacle by pouring alcohol down the fish's throat to encourage a more lively response. I thought the retired teacher Annie, who was an animal rights activist, was going to pass out over at the next table, the best I could do was try to avoid her distraught face.

Although the fish on our table has his tail to me I experience chilling unease at picking from a seemingly live prey but at such times I usually become philosophical. I wonder at how far removed we Westerners have come or think we have come from the predatory nature that is central to our human condition. I am more hypocritical than my Chinese hosts because I want the fish dead without any sign of life before I can eat. They are more true to the real nature of the predator which is to eat alive that of which it partakes.

The closing speech is given by the Head of the Department of Education, who like many senior Government officials in China is a woman. She acknowledges the contribution of teachers, students and DWA and welcomes future generations of foreign friends and workers to China. Amidst the applause my Chinese neighbour slightly the worse for 'bai jui' and feeling rather loose of tongue, miraculously begins to speak English and whispers seditiously to me,

' Now we are to call you 'foreign friends' instead of 'foreign devils.' I wonder how long this new policy will *to* last.'

' I hope for as long as I am in China', I reply uneasily.

'I drink to that,' he says cheerfully as he gives me the Chinese toast which translates as 'dry glass' and he proceeds to down the dregs of the fuming white spirit.

I decide to take advantage of the opportunity to see into a Chinese mind unbridled by caution or propaganda and ask why were we called foreign devils in the first place.

'When Chinese people first see 'out-side-country people,' the Chinese direct translation for foreigners, we think you look like ghosts - your skin so white and eyes so cold blue. So we call you 'Yang Guaize', which direct translation means 'Foreign Ghosts'. Then when the white ghosts start to carve up China between them as if we were a piece of cake and especially the English try to make the Chinese people opium addicts with the white powder from India we call the foreigners 'Foreign Devils.'

'I'm surprised that the Chinese government left us back in again.'

'Ah so, but the enemy of my enemy is my friend. Now the Soviet Union is not friendly with China so we are open the door to the United States and Europe. The Chinese peoples are a proud peoples because of our great culture and history. Only in the technology and the scientific today we are behind the West but soon we will learn from you what we need to developed. For this reason we now say welcome Foreign Friends.' So welcome Foreign Friend, may you live long in our Chila' and he toasts me again.

Although, initially I find the pragmatic attitude of my acquaintance quite alarming after stewing it around a while I recall the words of the Communist re-educator of Pu Yi, the last emperor of China. When Pu Yi accused him of keeping him alive only because he was useful to the Communists the re-educator replied, 'Is it such a crime to be useful to someone?'

The last few days in Beijing we feast our eyes on it's colour and movement.

As development workers we are to be posted to the poorer, more remote areas so it's a last opportunity to embrace Beijing's modernity and to buy many items that we had taken for granted in a capitalist society. Film, batteries, soap, toothpaste, shampoo, tampons, coffee, black tea, cheese, chocolate, sweets, clothes, shoes, books, video and cassette tapes will either be unavailable, of poor quality or not in Western sizes. We comb the markets for whatever items we consider to be most essential to us and what we can hope to carry.

Soon we will face the challenge of coping without. I feel it may be liberating to be freed from the clutter and preoccupation with material goods at least for a short period.

It's also comforting to know you can return to it all if you miss it. For now though there's a vital part of me that wants to put to the experiential test that well worn statement of my parents and many of their generation 'we were poor but we were happy.' Our allowance in China will be £50 a month. This is a very good wage we are told by Chinese standards. Our Chinese colleagues will be on £30 a month, but they also receive subsidies from the state for food and fuel which we are not entitled to.

This will be the last we are told we'll see of western-style fashions that have crept in despite Deng Xao Ping's vigilance. The last of young Chinese girls heavily made-up in mini-skirts and see-through blouses and guys in shorts and tee-shirts bearing Western advertising, sporting dark sunglasses and modern hairstyles like the 'feiji toe' or 'aeroplane look'. In the provinces the dress code is supposedly very conservative. It may be our only opportunity for some time to explore the sights and we attack them with gusto.

Tiananmen Square covering, over forty acres, dwarfs the droves of humans who go to visit it everyday. It is bounded by monumental buildings the most frequented of which is Chairman Mao's Mausoleum. Visitors file quickly past the embalmed wax-like corpse which looks impossibly large for a Chinese. But Mao was over six feet tall, another reason why he was admired by the normally petite Chinese. The main curiosity for a Western is witnessing the reverence with which the Chinese still behold their former leader. No words are uttered and the atmosphere is very solemn, almost religious.

The square forms the entrance to the more interesting Forbidden City which has all the bewitchment, secretiveness and intrigue of its reputation. Hall after magnificent hall capped by golden roofs reveal and conceal the treasures, the stories and the secrets of the generations which had made it their residence. The Temple of Heaven lies to the south of the Forbidden city and was conceived as the prime meeting point of heaven and earth.

At the Hall of Prayer for Good Harvests the Emperor prayed for abundance at the winter solstice. The Emperor played an important spiritual role in Chinese history. Only the Emperor could act as the mediator between heaven and the people. He interceded with his ancestors, the Celestial Court, and with Heaven itself by offering sacrifices on behalf of his people to amend any wrongdoing that may have been done the previous year. To this day the temple structure lends itself to otherworldly pursuits. Made entirely of wood without the aid of a single nail, it's towering, circular structure rising above a three-tiered marble terrace metaphorically attains the heavens through it's three blue tiled roofs. It feels like a place of transcendence that transports through its design, energy and location to a place beyond. Molly and I attract two volunteer guides, Guo Wei and Li Li, language students from the college, who are thrilled to exchange their company and knowledge for the opportunity to speak English.

'We have so little *the* opportunity to speak the real English with native *speakeurs* we are very happy to be with you,' says Guo Wei, a bubbling moon-faced twenty year-old girl from a Beijing suburb.

'My main *aumbition* is to study in abroad, improve my English and to make many foreign friends. China has been so *closid* from the outside countries for so long we are all very eager *for* to learn'

'Do you think you will be able to do so?' I ask.

'It depends on many things, first thing is my exam results, another thing if I can get the scholarship and finally if my parents and the Government agree.'

'Are you optimistic?'

'Yes, about my exam and my parents but not so sure about scholarship or the Government.

'Why is that?' Molly can't withhold her surprise.

'In *our Chila* scholarships very limited and the Government does not want too many of students going abroad. Many students go abroad they never come back. So only students with good connections, in Chinese we say 'guanxi', with the party are permitted. All the leaders children have studied in abroad and many do not come back.'

'Why so?' Now I'm surprised.

'They say more opportunities, better the standard of the life in abroad.'

'If we go to America,' interjects Li Li, an intense, twenty-two year old girl,

' we can have big car, beautiful house and very good job. Not so in *our Chila*.'

'Well, not everyone in America is rich.' I hasten to add.

'We heard that it is so - only the Government do not want us believe that so they write stories of Chinese too poor and *ashamdid* to come home. But we do not believe this - is Government propaganda. If things so bad in America why Government sons and daughters not come home?'.

'But Deng Xiao Ping's son lives in China.' pips Molly.

'Ah, yes but he is very wealthy man. He owns many businesses, joint ventures with foreign companies.

'Maybe you can also become successful here.' I suggest.

'*In our Chila* for success you must have very good connections.'

'In the west you have to make those connections too. And money often stays in the hands of the wealthy families, like the Royal Family in England.

'Still I must to find out for myself.'

'I'm sure you will Li Li'. I said.' But meanwhile life does not appear too difficult here in Beijing.'

'No, we are the lucky ones to be given *permissioun* to live here by the Government. Most people in *our Chila* want to live in Beijjng or in the cities along the east coast, but the government won't allow because there would be too many of people leaving the countryside.'

'So our students would really envy you.'

'Yes I think so because the standards and the *equipments* are much better here.'

'In my country too the people in the capital think things are better there but nowadays it is not true.'

'Believe me in Chila this *is a true*,' replies Li Li vehemently. 'The countryside is still very poor and underdeveloped. I know because my family are farmers from Guanxi province. Their life is very hard.'

We really appreciate Gou Wei and Li Li's frankness and sincerity and promise to help their English by writing to them. Although we regret leaving them and Beijing they give us a happy foretaste of the adventure that lies in the provinces. Saying goodbye to Molly is more difficult; we share the same nationality, humour and interests and would have been good mutual supports if we had been posted together. But that is not be our destiny, such matters were decided by DWA in London and we are resigned to our lot. We won't see each other again until the Chinese New Year, in February but we vow to write and telephone if possible. We are both hopeful that we will get along with our assigned colleagues, despite the sorry history of conflict between the two nationalities.

Chapter Three: Descendants of the Dragon.

'Oh, my God I'm really beginning to feel sick,' whispers Julie.

'Here's a bag - hang on in there,' I say, trying to sound reassuring, 'we'll be landing soon I'm sure.'

To be honest I can empathise with her queasiness - this is the third time the plane has taken an altitude dive in ten minutes. The prevailing joke is that CAAC, the abbreviation for China Airlines means 'China Airways Always Crashes.' Although the track record is really not that bad it's at times like this of course that the panic thoughts arise. Just hope there's not much more of this tummy churning turbulence. Just as I think this we begin to free-fall again for another couple of hundred feet. I can feel my insides hit the airplane ceiling as Julie starts to throw up into the bag.

I hand her some tissues and a bottle of water.

'Well at least we know it will be all down hill from here,' pops out before I can check myself but Julie manages a nervous laugh.

The Chinese passengers appear very unconcerned about the plane's gymnastic turns. Despite the lit up 'no-smoking' signs the whole plane is shrouded in smoke and butts are being thrown at a lively rate to the floor. No wonder they're not upset - nicotine-fixed the lot. Most of our travelling companions are men in Mao or western-style suits, probably travelling for business or official reasons. Whilst doing so they also manage to carry on board as many goods as possible, mostly in blue and white rope bags which are now clogging the aisles. So much for an emergency exit. The air hostesses don't seen to mind - probably because it saves them the bother of having to attend to the passengers on this veteran Soviet turbo prop. I've heard the Soviets are brilliant aircraft engineers but it doesn't help the nerves that all the signs are in Russian and the crew only speaks Chinese.

An older man on his way to the toilets at the back, clambering over the baggage, takes time to notice Julie's plight.

'Is your friend not well?' he asks in English. 'Here I give for you some Chinese traditional medicine for the upset stomach. I take it all times' and he hands over some small white tablets to me.

'That's really kind of you,' I reply 'we'll try it.' and to show my added appreciation I say 'thank you,' 'xie xie' effusively in Chinese.

'Can't do any harm Julie and could do a lot of good.'

She takes the pills and smiles a thank you at the man as he moves on.

Soon we seem to be 'plane'-sailing and Julie is recovering. We get a chance to notice the geography of northern China now that the plane's equilibrium has been restored. It is mountainous, ravenous and dessert-like at turns. Blue brown peaks give way to yellow ochre sand, green terraced slopes are fed by snaking rivers of silver. At times we seem to be flying precariously close to the mountain tops. I could reach out and almost touch them with my hands. But the Chinese passengers seem largely unperturbed by this.

Still I can't help wondering in a surreal kind of way how I would feel if it were all to end right now. Must be the altitude seeping into the brain cells. At least I've said farewell to everyone and I don't have any obligations left unfulfilled, or any debts owed. I have been very fortunate to come from such a close knit and loving family; to have had the opportunity to go to college, to travel. Still though I really wouldn't like to go this early in life. There's so much more I want to learn and experience especially now in China.

Living in the States was fascinating but in a way it was part of the same culture as Ireland. The same language, similar economic, political and philosophical systems. China is another universe. First there is the language to conquer. It is tonal like many other ancient languages, for example those found in Africa. The first inclination of humans must have been to sing rather than to speak and so great emphasis was put on the pitch of the sound as it is in singing. Modern Mandarin (the official language of China) has only five tones but in the south and in Hong Kong where Cantonese is spoken there are ten. In Mandarin the first tone is rising so you raise your voice at the end of the syllable, the second tone is falling so you lower your pitch at the end and so on for the high, medium and 'falling and rising' tones. The tone for the sound 'ma' for example can give five different meanings ranging from horse to mother. The derogatory word for a woman must be ' horse' rather than the 'cow' used in English.

As for the written language that's another ball game altogether. Instead of an alphabet the Chinese have characters and each character is a pictorial representation of a word or part of a word. The pictures that comprise the characters have been simplified and made more linear for writing which is why today most of them look abstract rather than representational. I reckon you have to have a very good visual memory to acquire the minimum three thousand necessary for literacy so for the moment I think I'll confine myself to the essentials needed for public signs and concentrate on the spoken language. After that I'll be on my way to understanding the customs and ways of the people. Then there is the political and economic system. It will be interesting to find out after experiencing the raw capitalism of the States how the controlled economy of the communists works in practice. And how a society which puts the community before the individual compares with a society which puts the individual at it's centre.

Of course I hope I have something to offer the Chinese, not only the English language training but my outlook and experience of life at the ripe old age of 26. Yet, somehow I have the feeling I will be learning as much if not more than what I teach. I'm sure for example the Chinese have progressed further than our modern analytical philosophy in the search for meaning in life. Surely there must be a greater answer to this question than the answer modern philosophy gives in the form of another question, 'i.e. that the question to be asked is not what is the meaning of life but what is the meaning of meaning.'

The meaning of meaning takes on a different perspective when the plane gives another belch and jolts us almost to the ceiling. Julie looks an unearthly colour and I think I must too.

'Please return to your seats immediately' announces the pilot. I'm amazed I can understand this rapid Chinese instruction - must be the lack of oxygen to the brain.

'As if we could possibly be conscious if we were anywhere else.' I try to relieve the breakpoint tension.

'Don't joke about it please' Julie pleads, ' I'm too nervous'

'Alright,' I agree to placate her though it's humour that keeps me sane in critical moments.

'I think he just said we are about to land' I offer soothingly.

'As if that's any consolation,' says Julie irritably.

I gauge from her mood that it's better to remain silent. Her anxiety distracts from my own and the next thing my mind meanders surreally philosophical again - western philosophy could only take me so far - it seemed to pose a lot more questions than it could answer. The quest for the meaning of life became the search for the meaning of meaning. Modern philosophy disappointed me because it has become more the study of language than an understanding of life. As a moral system it seemed to offer no new ideas. Maybe the Chinese philosophical system has something different to offer - a better moral system, more practical advice about how to live. Now I'll be able to see first hand. That's if this plane arrives safely.

At this moment it is hitting ground at a ferocious speed and Julie goes green and yellow beside me. I feel quite pink myself but the plane does not take off again suprise, suprise and we have landed. We follow the crowd around the back of a barn-type building made of concrete with a corrugated iron roof. Our baggage has been dumped in a clumsy heap to the ground and I am glad I have nothing fragile inside and sorry for those who have. A welcoming delegation of about ten have our names up on white cardboard signs and they appear very happy to see us.

'I am Mr. Lee,' says a pale lean man with a gracious manner.

'I am the director of Foreign Affairs and I am *responsibility* for your accommodation and other living needs, he says in a soothing soft voice. I hope you will have good stay here.'

'Thank you very much, we have been really looking forward to coming to Lanyuan University,' I respond eagerly. 'This is Julie and I'm Kayleigh as you have probably guessed from our application forms.'

'It is difficult for us Chinese to distinguish, especially from photos. Just so as many westerners find it difficult to tell one Chinese from another.'

'Actually I am already surprised at the variety of Chinese faces- much more than I expected - so perhaps I'll be able to identify you when I need you,' I tease.

'Auh so....I think in such situation no problem at all,' Mr. Lee laughs airily. 'Ah, but I must not be impolite, please allow me to introduce the Head of the Foreign Languages Department, Mr. Wu. His surname comes from the great Emperor Wu of the Han dynasty so it is fitting that he be a ruler', he says with a twinkle in his eyes.

'Welcome to *our Chila* and to our University,' says a big swarthy man with a sun - tanned melon face.

'*Accuse* me but my English is very poor, but I speak the Russia language very well. I know Miss Julie speak Russia good ' and he rockets off in Russian to a flustered Julie who responds in brief faltering tones. When finally she extracts herself from the steady stream, she turns to me relieved and translates as the others look on intently;

'I explained that my Russian is very rusty as its a few years since I've been there but from what I can gather Russian was the primary foreign language up until the 1980's. With the Open Door policy to the west English has become the main Foreign language so teachers like Mr. Wu have to change their subject at a late age. He says he thinks he is too old now to learn English well but because he is an experienced administrator he has been appointed head of our Department.'

'That's a good translation', says Mr. Lee. I also know Russian from college but fortunately I learned English at the same time. And so please allow me to introduce *for* you the others. This is Liang Dei Ru, one of our best teachers. Her name means butterfly and she likes to flutter around and be sociable.'

We shake hands with a tall broad young woman with warm cocoa eyes and an electric big-toothed smile.

'Never mind Mr. Lee, he is always joking a lot. If you have any problems with him come to me. I am very pleased to help you and I hope we will become fast friends. Here are two of your students Ming Wei and Mei Juan. They are from out of town so they are living on campus like you. I'm sure they will not leave you alone... no I mean ....lonely.'

The two smile coyly at us and welcome us to Lanyuan. Ming Wei looks older, with narrow eyes set in a narrow brown face framed by a neat bob. The other is more girlish with long raven hair, an elongated pretty moon face and a small bow mouth.

'This is Fang Yuan', says Mei Juan, 'he is also your student as well as being one of the drivers from the college.'

'You must be nice to him,' says Ming Wei, 'a driver is a very important job in *our Chila*. If you want to go anywhere by car you must ask him *permissioun*.'

'Thanks for the tip,' I smile, remembering the importance attached to smiling in Asia, 'pleased to meet you Fang Yuan.'

He is a weather-worn, medium height, wiry man in his thirties with an impish grin.

'Gaday,' he replies in an Australian accent much to Julie's and my astonishment.

'Did you live in Australia?' she asks.

'Yes, I worked on a sheep farm for two years in the outback.'

'Your English must be very good so,' Julie remarks.

'Yes, if you talk with me about rearing sheep or swear words, he laughs. but my reading and writing is very poor.'

'Well, I think we are ready to go now,' says Mr. Lee and with a gesture of the hand motions us to the awaiting white mini-bus. We all pile in and get a sore-bum ride on the pot-holed road into town.

For most of the ride we follow the river - this is at last - the glorious Yellow River- the cradle of Chinese civilisation. As early as the eight century BC the Chinese harnessed the power of the river for agricultural and trading purposes by building dikes and irrigation canals. The largest scheme was the building of the 1800 kilometres Grand Canal in the sixth century which connected the Yangzi and the Yellow rivers and was used to carry grain to the North. It was constructed using locks to control the water level - an innovation that did not appear in the west for another 400 years. Today river control is a huge operation; the river bed is dredged, diversion channels built, and reservoirs constructed on its tributaries. In addition the river has been forested to help prevent erosion and so keep the silt level down.

Here it is a mustard brown syrup worming its away across the elevated yellow earth squashed between the skyscraping cobalt blue mountains. Along its banks and half way up the terraced highlands are beehives of agricultural activity; tiny plots of land attended to with the tender loving care of individual gardeners, growing corn, cotton, hami and water melons and any other fruit or vegetables the land will host. Lanyuan is famous for the succulence of its melons our students reveal and the flavour has been improved by introducing varieties from the US.

Here in the North the dry harsh winter and the arid hot summers favour the cultivation of corn and wheat rather than rice. So, according to Mr. Lee, Xigan Province is also renowned for its noodles which come in all shapes, lengths and flavours. The really long ones which can be up to a metre length are served up on birthdays to ensure that the recipient will have a long life. The longer the noodle the greater longevity. Spinach, beans and eggs are included in the dough to give added nourishment and shapes like cats ears and nuns hats are moulded for variety.

'So we Chinese do not believe that the Italians invented noodles or indeed ice-cream' says Mr. Lee vehemently, 'instead Marco Polo came here and stole the ideas from us'

'Did Marco Polo come through Lanyuan then?' I venture.

'Yes Lanyuan was one of the towns along the silk road. They travelled over land rather than by river as the yellow river is not navigable for long distances.'

'Yes it looks incredibly muddy here,' says Julie.

'It is,' says Mr. Lee,' it is the muddiest river on the earth because of the loess soil through which it runs. Every year it carries one and a half million tonnes of silt to the sea and this causes the river to flood and even change direction. In some places the river rises from 15 to 30 feet higher than the surrounding land.'

'Not in Lanyuan, I hope,' Julie interjects.

'No, thankfully not in Lanyuan bur further down stream there have been many flooding disasters. The river has been kind to Lanyuan; it has provided irrigation and crops to an area that would otherwise surely be dessert. This is why we in China have great respect for the river. It was along the Yellow River that our earliest ancestors settled. Because of its power and it's temperament we often refer to the Yellow River as a dragon. And we are the descendants of the dragon who rose up out of the yellow soil of the river. To the river we are grateful for the lovely yellow skin of girls like Mei Juan.'

'And to the yellow sun we are grateful for the black skin of Fang Yuan,' the driver adds with a shout and the whole bus rises into a round laugh.

'Come on Fang, sing the song *Descendants of the Dragon* to welcome our guests.' enthuses Lee and the rest of the bus egg him on.

His voice is surprisingly voluminous and melodious and as the others join in we make a rollicking garrulous arrival at the University.

The entrance is an impressive concrete archway enveloping large iron gates with the University name written in majestic red calligraphy. A wide paved laneway leads onto a symmetrically planned campus with large concrete blocks, some up to ten storeys high, separated by walkways and miniature rock and flower gardens. We pass a large sports field where volleyball, badminton and soccer are being played. The car comes to a standstill in front of a large two-storey building which Mr. Lee tells us is the Foreign Guest House.

'You will be staying here in the time being.'

In the time being means how long, I wonder, and I look at Julie to see her reaction. We were told by DWA that we would integrated into University life from the start and so we would be housed in an apartment on campus with the Chinese staff as were the previous foreigner teachers. Julie looks slightly askance.

At the reception area Mr. Lee, Mr. Wu and the others take their leave but instruct the two female students to remain to assist us. We are ushered upstairs to a hotel style apartment with a large living area off of which there are two bedrooms and a bathroom. The walls, thank heavens, are painted magnolia rather than the ubiquitous medical green but the paint job is shoddy and peeling. Lime nylon carpets have been let fall on the floor revealing the original concrete along the gartered edges. There is an empty roughly plastered room with a pane of glass looking onto the living room. Ming Wei and Mei Juan tell us that it is to be a kitchen. I wonder why a kitchen in a hotel room but they don't seem to know either.

I offer Julie the larger bedroom, we dump our bags and take the girls up on their offer of a guided tour of the campus.

It's massive; facilitating and housing over 11 million students and staff. The student accommodation is austere and dismal. The hallways and stairways are unpainted, dimly lit and laden with pools of water. The bathrooms are a dank disgrace and cesspools of disease. Trickles of cold water flow to concrete wash basins- the only source of washing water. The loos are tiled gullies with an obvious restriction on water supply judging from the rank stench.

The dormitories themselves have been humanised by habitation; the gentle touch of Chinese femininity in the women's dorm where pastel pink and blue mosquito nets have been deftly hung from metal bunks embracing the visitor in an oriental mystique. Calendar pictures of pink faced boys and girls sporting the latest fashions and hairstyles from Hong Kong adorn the unpainted walls.

We are introduced to some more of our female students and are surprised that they seem older than the 18 upwards that we expected our middle school trainee teachers to be.

'But we are not trainee teachers, says Ming, 'we are professionals who have come here to improve our English. Most of us want to do the TOEFL or EPT examinations so we can go to the abroad to study.

'I've never heard of those examinations before,' says Julie.

'The TOEFL is the American test of English as a foreign language,' I explain, 'but I've never heard of the EPT.'

'Oh, that is the Chinese Government test it is quite similar to the TOEFL, except there are often mistakes even in the answers because the Chinese teachers who make the exam do not have the correct English.' Ming's face expands into a grin.

'I can see we will have some fun trying to give the wrong answer to the wrong questions.' I chuckle.

The girls giggle.

'We heard the Irish people have the sense of humour but the English have a stiff upper lip. Is that really so?' Mei's eyes look impish.

'Ah we wouldn't like to spoil the suprise of getting to know us by giving you an answer to that question, now would we Julie?' I wink at Julie.

'Of course not,' respond Julie, 'though feel free to test my lips.'

Amid the laughter I ask Ming Wei if she knows if we are to teach any Middle School trainee teachers as outlined in our contract. She says as far as she knows we are to teach on the fee paying course for professionals who wish to do further study.

'Fee paying, you mean you're paying to do this course?'

I have not yet acquired the Chinese habit of hiding my emotions. Ming and Mei's eyes register my suprise.

'Well most of us are being paid for by our work unit but some are paying for themselves.' Ming's tone is formal.

'That's strange. We were told by our organisation that we would be teaching the Middle school teachers who come from the poor parts of the countryside. DWA is a charity, providing people free of charge, to work with the poor. There must be some misunderstanding.'

'I think you must to discuss with Mr. Lee and Mr. Wu.' Says Ming evading my eyes. Mei's eyes are vacant. Two immovable Chinese mountains.

We have a 'banquet' at seven with the Head of the college, Mr. Lee and Mr. Wu. At this stage we already know that when the Chinese say banquet they mean banquet so we leave our stomachs empty for the evening avalanche ahead. Julie and I discuss whether to bring up the subject of our slightly manipulated job descriptions and opt for the local custom; if a gate is opened we enter if it's closed we do not knock, at least not yet.

'We have never had the Irish teacher before you must tell us about your country,' Mr. Wu enthuses presidentially at the top of the table. He is surprisingly well fed for a Chinese - his big belly almost touching his plate. Although he's smiling there is a dark impenetrability about his eyes. Something I cannot discern makes me feel uncomfortable with him. This unease is augmented by the formality of the occasion . Instead of the usual cosy equalising round table there is an elongated type more typical of a boardroom.

I decide its an occasion to give my ambassadorial speil and I address the table;

'Well, it's a small island with a population of 4 million. It is made up of 32 counties. 26 form the Republic of Ireland which is independent and six form Northern Ireland which is part of the United Kingdom.'

'Oh, that's the place where all the boom is.' Mr Lee's eyes light up his comment.

'Yes, there still is some trouble there but the different governments are trying to sort it out.'

'So there won't be any boom boom between you and Julie.' Mr. Wu guffaws to the group.

'Well, not over politics anyway, eh Julie.'

'Definitely not, I have no interest,' and she turns from me to the others, 'but they do say the Irish have hot tempers.'

'Oh, that's only if they are provoked,' I chuckle.

'Well, we hope you are not easily provoked then because in China it is big loss of face to loose your temper in public.' There was a warning in Liang Dei Ru's voice.

I really was not expecting this directness from my colleagues. We had been given the impression by DWA that the Chinese were indirect and circular in their communication.

'Yes, the last DWA teacher was not so popular because she often lost her temper in class, the attendance was very poor.' Liang Dei Ru's face looked older without the electric smile.

'Well, I wouldn't consider it appropriate to loose my temper in class.' I try to add reassurance to my voice.

'Ah so ...it is good to get these things clear from the beginning. We have had many misunderstandings with our

foreign teachers in the past,' Mr Lee explains lightly.
'Especially about relations with the students. We have lost some of our finest students to foreign teachers.'

'So we have heard, but you needn't worry on that score,' Julie looks very definite, 'we both have boyfriends at home.'

'Definitely out of the question very unprofessional in my opinion.' I add in a tone of absoluteness.

'Oh, we are very relived to hear that,' says Mr Lee, 'we find that once the girls had their boyfriends they were not interested in their work.'

'Oh, we are very sorry to hear that but we can assure you that will not be the case with us. We are really looking forward to working hard.' I hope that I haven't overdone the sincerity but sensing that a gate has been opened I enter;

'Since you are being so frank with us.... we were wondering if our job description has been changed. We were under the impression from DWA that we were to be teaching the Middle School trainee teachers from the countryside who have no opportunity of having foreign teachers.'

Mr. Wu seems a bit confused by my question and turns to Mr. Lee for a translation. After a bit of conflaboration Mr. Lee turns to us to say;

'This semester you are to teach on the short term fee paying course for professionals. This is because we already have two American teachers teaching the Middle School trainee teachers.'

Julie and myself look at each other quite flabbergasted at this.

'But says Julie, 'it is DWA policy to send us to the institutions with the greatest need and normally that means a college without other foreign teachers.'

'Well,' says Mr Lee, with the caution of a skater on ice, 'we weren't expecting any other teachers but ULS, the American organisation sent us two free teachers. They arrived before you so we assigned them the trainee teachers classes.'

'But have you informed DWA about this?' I ask,

astonished.

'Not yet, but we intend to,' came the lame response.

'You understand that we will be obliged to as well.' Julie strikes this dead between his eyes.

'Yes, of course, as you wish..... but meanwhile we would like you to be in class on Monday. Liang Dei Ru and Mr. Wu will assist you with the timetable and materials.

'We are ready when you are.' Julie responds.

'Very well. Over the weekend the students will assist you in settling into your apartment ... buying household goods and a bicycle etceteras etceteras. Mr Lee's formal tone has some ring of the amusement of Yul Brenner in the King and I.

'So we'll be moving into our new apartment at the weekend then?' I enthuse.

'Auh so, ...ahem...it seems that the previous apartment occupied by DWA teachers is now being occupied by the Vice President Mr. Zhou, our Vice president who has just returned from the US... So you are to stay in the Foreign Guest House apartment. Don't be troubled we will get equipment for your from your DWA grant.'

'As you probably know it is DWA policy to house teachers in similar accommodation to their Chinese counterparts so that they can integrate into Chinese society as much as possible. We would be concerned that this might be difficult if we are to remain in the Foreign Guest house. Is it possible that another apartment may be available the staff quarters.' Julie adopts Mr Lee's formality to hide her obvious disappointment.

Mr. Lee discusses again with Mr. Wu and the Vice President in Chinese and then turns to say,

'I am afraid there is nothing else available right now. We have a very big demand on housing. We all agree that the Foreign Guest House is quite suitable. You can come and go as you please except of course the front door closes at eleven. When we get you kitchen equipment you can cook for yourself. In the mean time you will buy meal cards to eat in the dinning room. You will also have the company of the American teachers.' Mr. Lees face is as adamant as his words.

I see the disappointment swell up in Julie's face and I'm sure mine betrays the same emotion as I glibly acknowledge our respective fates with

'I see.'

Our Chinese hosts appear nonchalant about the whole affair but I wonder if in time we will be able to read their faces as easily as we can read our own. Or are they really as inscrutable as they are reported to be by other Westerners? The emphasis put on loss of face must contribute to this but when you think about it we do have similar customs in the Occident; like giving a good impression, and no public displays of affection. Anyway I decide not to pursue the issues further as the gates seem very definitely closed.

The conversation moves on to less prickly issues like the local specialities in food and the sights to be seen around Lanyuan and the evening ends quite pleasantly with the men rolling home after the required Baijui. As we later discover the entertainment of Foreign guests is often used as a good opportunity to delve into the expense account.

Chapter four: Eggs for sale.

'Yi, er, san, si, wu, liu,' (one, two, three, four, five, six) the Early Morning Exercise Programme on the College PA shouts us from the landscape of dreams into the lemon and lime light of a Northern Chinese autumn morning. I have had a turbulent night sleep after mulling over with Julie what to do about the change in our conditions. We decided to write to Rupert at DWA but besides being posted to a different institution we couldn't envisage any other solution. During the night my conscience was addled by the fact that we had been posted to a relatively wealthy college which already had foreign teachers doing our work when there could be others in more dire need. Yet I didn't want to start all over again next semester in a new college.

In deeper sleep my dreams were in water world and I was playing underground volley ball with my new Chinese acquaintances. As I jumped above the net my head and those of the others emerged above water level and slowly they began to metamorphose into the heads and bodies of my family and friends in Ireland. I was trying to exploring the meaning of this symbolism when my thoughts were pelted by the noise so I tumbled out of bed to get dressed. Just as well, Ming and Mei were already at the door scrubbed, alert and shoe shined.

'We will take you to the college noodle shop for breakfast. Lanyuan speciality, *nu rou mian*....English translation beef noodles... and then we will take you down town for shopping and playing.' Ming's tone has the resonance of authority characteristic of many teachers.

'Playing,' I ask, 'playing what?'

'Just playing.... don't you say *playing* in English to mean *to enjoy yourself*.'

'In English we use *play* in connection with children usually. For adults it depends, we would normally say what the activity is for example in this case *sight seeing* or more generally we would say *to have fun* or *enjoy ourselves.*'

'Oh, thank, thank you, we want you to correct our English very much, we are very eager to learn and to go abroad.' Both Ming and Mei trip over each others words to show their appreciation.

'Your English is very good already but I will help you as much as I can.' It's reassuring to see the girls are emotional about something and of course its also nice to feel needed.

'Oh thank you so much.' They garble on.

Already by seven o'clock the noodle shop is packed. It is bare and essential: a stained whitewashed, rectangular room, with wooden tables and stools and a counter of steam at the top from which the pressurised cooks are dolling out noodles from witches cauldrons. Behind them are among the most industrious workers in China; the noodle makers, kneading out the dough, cutting it into strips which they then hold between outstretched hands. Then as if by some magical motion they manage to elongate the strips into lengths longer than any python. We have a choice of thick noodles, thin noodles, white or yellow and I opt for what the students suggest, knowing I'll have the time to try them all. A perspiring face supporting a white decked body throws our choice into a bowl of clear soup, topped with coriander and the skimpiest slices of beef. I am advised by Ming to buy *quaize* (chopsticks) and when we see those on offer in the dirty jars on the table we can see why. Hepatitis is very common in China and with wooden chopsticks attracting germs one can understand why.

'Hu Yao Bong wants the Chinese to use knives and forks instead of chopsticks.' Ming says matter of factly.

'Who is Hu Yao Bang?'

'He is one of our great leaders. He wants to improve the conditions in education and for the minority people. He even wants to free Tibet and bring more democracy to China.'

'He sounds very radical does he have much support?'

'Yes particularly from the intellectuals. What do you think of these ideas?' Ming eyes me so intently that for a moment her black fringe seems to frame the face of a spy. Then I think that's just paranoia but just in case I veer away from the political.

'I don't think I'd like to see chopsticks disappear particularly since I've just learnt how to use them. The disposable ones seem pretty safe and so do the plastic and metal ones.'

Is Ming taking mental notes of what I am saying but before I can ponder her expression Mei interjects:

'You will find because you are left handed you will have difficulty in China. Your elbow will become like a sword to the person next to you.'

'Isn't anyone in China left handed?' My voice belies my amazement.

'Oh yes... lots of people are but our Chinese custom is to use the right hand for chopsticks.' Ming's voice re-echoes its previous authority.

'I'm afraid it's a bit too late for me to change now. Luckily I have small arms. But what do Chinese people think of left-handed people.'

'Oh,......they think they are lucky and clever. Nowadays many of our famous calligraphers are left handed though in the past they were not allowed to write with the left hand.' Mei is eager to divulge.

Despite the slurping, gurgling sounds of the eaters and the dark Dickensian atmosphere the soup is delicious. The atmosphere is abetted by the hawking sound of spit being drawn up from the darkest recess of the chest up along the well worn oesophagus to be retched, yanked out of the throat onto the floor which has become a spittoon bowl. The *No Spitting* signs look down with the pitiful gaze of the ignored.

'The regular buses are filled up at this hour on a Saturday. I think we will have to take the number eleven,' says Mei in a jolly way.

'Does that go down town too?' I ask.

Mei and Ming erupt into giggles.

'The number eleven is the Chinese way of saying let's go and walk because the two number ones look like a person's legs. But it is too far to walk - at least six li.' Ming obviously enjoys explaining things to her foreign teacher, to show off her English and her profession.

'That's about six kilometres is it?'

'Yes.....oh but here comes a Xiao Mian Bao, lets get that.' Ming takes control again.

A *xiao mian bao* is Chinese slang for a minibus, literally a small wheat bun. They are about three times the cost of the public bus but they are quicker since they don't stop everywhere and normally you can get a seat. They are another product of the liberalisation of the economy. Private transport run at a profit, they appear to be racking in the customers. They are a two-person operation, a driver and a people shover and collector of currency. Enterprising as they are they try to extract Foreign Exchange currency from us but the students insist on telling them we are teachers working at the University and are therefore authorised to use local currency or renmenbi.

FEC or Foreign Exchange Certificates were introduced by the Chinese Government to control the amount of foreign currency and imports in the country. To buy foreign goods required FEC which are supposed to be of the same worth as local currency but in reality are of higher value as exchange is restricted by the authorities. As a result there is a thriving black market in FEC which can often be worth twice the value of The Peoples Money. Since we are residents rather than tourists we are allowed to use either.

Down town we join the Yellow River again. There is a promenade leading down to a pier where the Muslim boats are set assail. The bulk of the Muslim quarter is across the river and I promise Ming to go another time and *play*.

Islam took root in China in the seventh century where it was introduced by traders, mercenaries and sailors from Persia and the Arabian Peninsula. It's strongest adherents reside in the Northwest and the Southeast seaports. The Muslims intermarried and converted some of the Han Chinese (the dominant Ethnic group) and they became known as the Hui. Because they also embraced a number of the major ethnic groups, including the Turkish people of the Northwest they are regarded as one of the 55 ethnic minorities, which make up about seven percent of the population of China. The minorities are small in number (around six million) but significantly occupy about sixty percent of the land area. Because of the low density of their populations these people are excepted from the one child policy.

I am content to view the egg cup upside down roofs of the mosques and the skull caps of the men from the left bank. The more serious work of looking for a good bike is at hand and we have our first real taste of *the iron rice bowl* at its worst and the real reasons why Deng Xiao Ping had to turn it on its side if not upside. The iron rice bowl refers to the Chinese system of state employment. Generally the state provided work for everyone and the same level of payment no matter what her individual contribution. The rice was always there no matter how hard you worked. This had led to the lowest common denominator in terms of input and output. People were discouraged from making an effort by their colleagues and by a system that gave no monetary reward for enterprise or hard work. By the time Deng Xiao Ping had introduced his reforms in 1986 factory and agricultural production was minimal.

Introducing a capitalist system with incentives had lead to increased industrial output and farmers who could now sell their surplus in the free markets were much more productive. This however had lead to increased apathy among those in state employment which included those in the big department stores where bicycles were sold

It was very difficult to get attention at the huge Peoples department store. The women were sitting behind the counter chatting and knitting. When we asked if we could look at the bicycles they said they were only for display purposes not for sale. Ming and Mei said this was their way of avoiding work they were not interested in. We were obliged to go to another store which was privately owned.

Even here we were faced with the dilemma of which crock to choose from. The store owner who was very interested explained to us that all the best equipment was shipped out of China for export and we were left with the second rate. He sold us the bikes with the least amount of problems and Ming and Mei bargained him down to a reasonable price. Outside on the streets one of the many bicycle repair men did a cheap and efficient job on both our bicycles. We got on our bikes and experienced the luxury of private transport Chinese style once again.

Monday morning our escorts Ming and Mei arrive at seven thirty. The more energetic students are exercising in the sports field outside Dean Wu's office. Instead of finding the usual shelves piled high with books of an academic office Dean Wu greets us behind an avalanche of chicken eggs. His big watermelon face cracks into a yellow toothed grin as he asks with the audacity of a street trader if we would like to buy some.

'They come from the countryside, are very fresh, cheaper than the market, only 6 Kuai a jin.'

Funny how Dean Wu's English dramatically improves when he talks money.

'When Mr. Jia buys our new cooker' I respond with an innocent smile.

'Meanwhile, would it be possible to see what reading materials you have. DWA said that they bought quite a number of text books.'

'Unfortunately many of the students kept them for themselves so we only have this box left.' Mr Wu has started to light his pipe with the slow pace of a man who doesn't care whether the whole university collapsed around him. What was left in the box was dismal, a few games books.

Fortunately Julie and I had brought a number of books from Beijing with our DWA equipment grant but what were we to do for supplies for the students? We are shown a Jetstener, a mini printing machine which requires materials to be typed on an original stencil, from which copies can be made . We are also told we can get copies of most textbooks in the Foreign Language Bookstore. Mr Wu generously offers to make tapes for the students at the meagre price of 10 Yuan, one tenth of the average monthly wage. He inhales deeply and emits a smoky smile.

I try to perform one of those inconsequential smiles of social smoothness I have seen worn already by my Chinese acquaintances and ask about the whereabouts of

the tape recorders provided last year by DWA. These also seem to have mysteriously disappeared without a ruffle to Mr. Wu's indifference. Meanwhile we can use the office ones which Mr Wu informs us with a puff of his pipe are not in great condition. He is very repetitive in his encouragement of us obtaining the latest models from our DWA allowance.

For the more tedious task of assigning our duties Mr Wu reverts to Ming's interpretation.

Classes will be from 8-12 o'clock Monday to Friday. We will also be available in our office in the afternoon to assist students. We may also be required to do voice-overs on promotional videos for the University as well as tapes and videos for Chinese students to learn Chinese. The latter tasks have not been mentioned in our job description but we both agree out of interest and to appear willing to co-operate.

Dean Wu informs me that he will be attending my first class. I am not too unduly concerned about this as I have an interesting slide show of my family and country prepared. The class are suitably entertained and at the end of the session I leave questions opened to the floor. The torpedo of inquiries on every subject impels me to keep a mental note to restrict the subject matter in the future.

'How old are you?' asks a young man dressed in Western style with an impish grin.

'I thought Mr. Wu had told you all that already' I wink mischievously at the group.

The classroom walls quiver with mild laughter.

But the young rogue is persistent, 'Mr. Wu did not tell us.'

'It isn't customary for Western people to freely discuss their age and anyway I think I am far too old for you.' This time the walls rebound with musical laughter.

Relieved to have dodged the embarrassment of revealing my age in public I was totally unprepared for the next assault which came from behind and left me reeling for a while.

'Why are you not married?' the speaker of all people is Fang Yuan, the driver.

I take a deep breath and clutch the podium for support.

'Well, Fang Yuan I understand that you have lived abroad......... In Australia I believe?' I smile to recover my composure, but my jaw feels stiff. How can the Chinese produce their smiles so effortlessly. I am told there is a smile to cover every social situation from embarrassment to elation.

Fang Yuan is not diverted. 'Yes I lived in Australia but why do you ask?'

'Was it the custom there to ask women that question?'

'Sure, no problem.' he pipes up with a jocular grin.

'Well, I must say I'm surprised because it is not the custom in my country unless you know the person pretty well. It is a personal question but to give you a general answer. In my country people who go to University usually marry later in life mostly for financial reasons.'

'But do you have a special friend?' Fang Yuan's face takes on the expression of a cheeky monkey.

'Oh I have many special friends, don't you?'

The group chortles again but Yuan has the persistence of a stubborn child pestering his mother for sweets.

'I mean do you have a boyfriend?'

'Why are you so curious?' At this stage I have to forcibly restrain myself from putting my hands on my hips.

'Oh I think everybody is *interesting* this question.' Fang Yuan was definitely born in the Chinese Year of the Monkey.

'But this is a private question.'

'Not in our Chila..... it is a public question'

'Well to end the issue, yes,' I say feeling my voice reverberate forcibly. 'Are you happy now?'

'Yes happy to have an answer but and not so happy with the answer' and his bold dark face reveals no trace of embarrassment.

An older thickset woman pipes up,

'Never mind Yuan, you can do better than him. Mr Tui here,' she points to a burly soft faced man beside her, 'is a *matchermaker* he can make you a good match.

A Chinese husband is much better than an Irish husband, he is *vely* good cook and housekeeper and *vely* caring.'

'Thank you very much for offering and by the way it's known as a matchmaker' and I write on the board to divert attention to the learning aspect of the lesson. 'In the West matchmakers have been replaced by dating clubs and computer dating. Besides Mr. Wu would be very upset if he thought that I was spending my time looking for a husband and not attending to my duties.'

Bubbles of laughter again though this time I notice not everyone is laughing. This I attribute to different levels of comprehension of the language rather than any lack of humour.

At last the questioning follows the less sensitive pathway of wealth and property.

They are genuinely surprised to learn that not everyone in the West is rich, not everyone has their own house and own car and they never figured on the cost of living being so high.

I don't think they are quite convinced by my answers either. I think they think I am just perpetuating the Government propaganda that all is not well in the West because I am partly in Government employment

'Why did you come to a poor country like China?' there is an odour of suspicion about the question from an older reserved-looking gentleman and when I reply that I have always been fascinated by the older and wiser East his expression remains doubtful. He must think I am one of those Western Marxist sympathisers here for ideological reasons.

Other questions are more humane and mundane

'Do you miss your family?' asks a young girl with a sympathetic face.

'Well, I've only just arrived but I 'm sure I will.'

'Is it always raining and foggy like London...... .like we read in Charles Dickens?' asks a young man with coke bottle glasses.

'Now that you mention it the weather is one of the favourite subjects in Ireland but the most reliable thing you can say about our weather is that it is unreliable which is why we talk about it a lot. It is always changing so we have lots to talk about. To answer your question it rains a lot but not very heavy and there is not much fog.'

Then the questions broach the favourite Chinese subject of food. They are very curious to know what cheese tastes like but not that keen to eat it because they think it will make them smell like a cow.

Then there are the quirky childlike questions based on the assumption that we Westerners are aliens from another planet

'Why are Western men so hairy?'

And all I can think of to respond is:

'Why are Chinese men not hairy?' which provokes a chuckling response from the majority.

Then there are the naughty questions or are they purely innocent?

'What is a French letter?' The man looks seriously respectable but who knows. I respond in my super formal teacher mode:

'It's not suitable for discussion in English class.'

'Can we come to your bedroom to ask you questions.' I gauge from the naive face of the young man standing that this is a perfectly innocent mistake.

So I set about explaining;

'Normally students would not come to a teachers bedroom, you would come to the living room. In my case you may come to the office during office hours.'

Ming Wei is again thrilled with the opportunity to explicate in a deliberate way

'In *Chila* often the person's bedroom and living room are the same room.'

'Thank you Ming Wei for your assistance,' and seizing the opportunity to take control of the situation, I address the class;

'Now I would like to ask you some questions to see how much you have understood. After that I will put you in pairs with someone you don't know and ask you to interview each other.'

From my questioning I am surprised to find the comprehension level varies a lot. So I will have to inform Dean Wu that there will be a need to divide the class according to competency. Wonder how he'll react to that.

The interview session is only partly successful. The students are not familiar with the Communication Method of learning English. They are reluctant to speak as they are used to sitting in class and listening to the teacher do all the talking. I explain to them that the more they speak the better they will get. Speaking is like any other skill -practice makes perfect. They are impressed with the cliché and ask me to write it up on the board.

However when I begin to circulate to listen to their conversation they speak directly to me rather then their fellow

student. When I ask them why this is so they protest plaintively, almost in usion
'We want to hear you speaking not the other student. His English is only the same level as ours....is *vely* poor.'
I assure them that their standard of English is good and explain that in real life situations abroad they will often be speaking to non native speakers so it is still good practice for them. They can learn from each other by practising together. I point out the physical impossibility of the teacher speaking to everyone individually and at the same time. And although they recognise the logic of the situation still they are like children craving attention such is their voracious thirst for learning, hanging off the teacher's every word, competing for her approval. Their puppy dog naiveté in thinking that each one is your only student and their individual learning is the teacher's sole responsibility contrasts with their communal upbringing and obvious intelligence. The incongruity of this is to strike me more as I venture deeper into the culture. Perhaps all cultures and personalities have this mix of innocence and knowledge, individuality and community.

Chapter five: Chi Hai O.

It is surprising in retrospect that I ever had time or space for romance. We were after all under continuous surveillance by the Foreign Affairs Unit of the University through its extensive net. This web included the Director, Mr. Lee and his assistant, Mr Yang, Mr. Wu, our Dean and *the sticky backs* Ming Wei and Mei Juan, as we nicknamed them. Whether the latter two were specifically assigned by Foreign Affairs we were never completely sure - what was certain was that none of the other students appeared to intrude on their territory - they seemed to have special rights to us. Neither were we certain that they were spies in the official sense. Mostly they appeared to us to be the last vestiges of that massive spy web of the terrible Great Cultural Revolution which ensnared every member of society. A lot of students confided suspicion of each other to a lesser or greater degree and many seemed to trust us more than their own people.

Everywhere we turned, however, *the sticky backs* seemed to be there. Offering us help with negotiating every aspect of Chinese life, from going to the post office to shopping, from cooking to our relationship with other Chinese.

Ming in particular attached herself to me and had an opinion on everyone before I even met them. She seemed to deliberately separate herself from the others in an imperious, patronising manner. It was obvious she was not liked for this but it did not appear to bother her. In the beginning she developed my sympathy for her by telling me her story. Her husband divorced her because their one child was a girl not a boy. He remarried and his new wife had produced the right sex. Later when I began to know her better I wondered if this was truly the only reason. It was not an official ground for divorce and divorce was extremely difficult to obtain.

Whatever the whole story her life experience had embittered her towards men and she gossiped voraciously about the other students relationships. For this reason I tried to distance myself from her. It wasn't easy. She was a limpet. The system had given her exclusive rights to be my chaperone and in the early days when I was still grappling with the language and the culture her practical help was almost indispensable.

Mei Juan was Julie's barnacle but they seemed to strike up a more sincere friendship. She was more fun loving and optimistic and less politically correct. Mei Juan confided in Julie that Ming Wei was jealous of her because she was younger and more pretty and had many admirers. She had been a dancer with an ethnic dancing group and had already travelled the world until an injured foot broke her career. Learning English was a passport to work in business in one of the Free Economic Zones in the South. When she trusted us more she gave us a more intimate account of her story. The broken leg was the excuse. The real reason was personal. She was in love with the lead dancer and he loved her too. However the leader of the dance troupe, an older man, had taken a fancy to him and used his position to coerce him into an affair with him. The young star felt he had no choice but to succumb for the sake of his career and Mei Juan left the troupe because of a broken heart.

The intensity of our relationships with Ming and Mei was compounded by the intensity of our work and the students insatiable hunger for English. We were quickly learning how the personal life could be eliminated in China. We were assigned extra classes on tap and extra duties which included editing scripts, voice-overs for TV programmes, and producing English language tapes for radio. There seemed to be a student from any department at our door any free time we had, looking for help with anything from an University application form to homework. Eventually exhaustion forced us to call a halt to it and confine them to office hours.

Even our social life was dictated by work. We were invited to students homes or on outings only to find we were extending the language lesson. For this reason I guarded my Chinese language and drawing classes with great jealousy as they were the only personal pursuits I was allowed.

I loved the Chinese water colour and ink painting of landscapes and that love led me to the love of my life. My art teacher invited me to the opening of an exhibition and I got the time wrong. Was it an accident or an event waiting to happen? Are all accidents predestined? Is destiny accidental? Is that after all the message of the I Ching. Anyway it was a happy accident.

He was humorous and that was an excellent start.

'If you move any closer you will be in the picture,' his grins up to the sparkle in his eyes. He was a Marx brothers fan.

'I think I would like to be it's so heavenly.' and I sneak a sideways glance at the figure who has sent a heat wave through my body.

'Well it is my impression of heaven, but I should have waited until I met you then it would have been complete.' says this dark stranger with exquisite features and exotic eyes.

Later at the close of the exhibition we were standing side by side and he was holding my coat..

'We seemed to have ended up together.' I felt awkward despite my pretended aloofness.

'I would have thought that was by intention.'

'Really on your part???... I was just letting the evening carry me.' I try hopelessly to affect the on screen nonchalance of Gretta Garbo.

'That is a form of choice too you know.'

'Yes I do ....'

I wonder how he felt.

The wizardry of fiction-here is how.

Chi Hai O

I couldn't believe she was looking at my paintings with such interest. And what did she see in them with Irish green eyes speckled with yellow like a wild bird's eggs.

I was so full up with her I couldn't see anything else in the room. Hair the colour of wheat fields in May falling in waves around her head dazzled my eyes from behind. And then she turned to look at me her face bewitched me. Her eyes sent out a laser light that fixed mine to hers. The contour of her lips as her soft speech outlined seductive shapes that I had never before witnessed. Her skin was baby white and sun kissed with freckles. What had I done to deserve to see this vision? I don't know how I kept standing. It must have been a higher source than myself. Amazingly I was able to laugh and joke. She must have thought I was very cheeky

She is singing, humming to herself as I come up behind her staring into my painting.

'If you move any closer you will be in the picture,' I joke hoping she knows the Marx brothers.

'I think I would like to be it's so heavenly' and she doesn't look around

'Well it is my impression of heaven.'

'What you are the artist?' and she turns around to look at me for the first time I will never forget the first look I have of her face; the shiny porcelain skin, the radiant green eyes, her peach lips and divine smile. I feel bewitched. Transfixed. I cant' find words for a while when she says:

'You're the artist? It's superb, brilliant. Congratulations on the exhibition and she extends her hand to congratulate me.

All I can manage at first is a thank you in my native tongue.

She continues.

'Chi Hai O isn't it. I'm sure that name has a deep meaning.'

'Well Chi is the Chinese word for energy. And Hai O means seagull. My father saw a flock of them the day I was born.'

'So your art has the energy of the sea.'

'Perhaps.'

'But it's such a curious mixture of styles. I can see the Chinese tradition in the landscape but then the figures are almost abstract in a Western way. The colour composition is a mixture of Chinese inks and delicate water colours. Yet there are more vibrant colours, reminiscent of Guagain.'

'I've been very influenced by Western art though naturally exposure here is rather limited,' I mutter, 'but you seem very knowledgeable about art.'

'I've always loved art. lately I have been taking Chines landscape painting classes. I find it fascinating, almost meditative.'

'Yes at its deepest level it is a form of meditation. But I am truly sorry I didn't know you before I drew my heaven I feel it is not complete without you.'

She blushes.. 'You are very flattering.'

'No no...not flattering, truthful.' and I realise I am staring at her and I have embarrassed her. To divert I ask.

'Do you realise the exhibition doesn't start till nine?'

'Really..... Ge Yan told me to meet her hear at eight. I was wondering what was keeping her.'

'That's all right I can use the time to give you the guided tour if I may.'

'You are too kind but I'm sure you have preparations to do.'

'This will be my preparation.'

And I delighted in showing her my mind, my dreams, my visions, my soul.

And she entered my world and seemed so much a part of it that I felt she had always been there. I wondered where we had met before and for the first time truly believed in reincarnation and past lives.

It seemed natural that we would walk home together after the exhibition and we found each other easily. I could not remain unconscious of her energy in the room her light was so radiant. I hardly noticed how successful the exhibition had been with offers to buy and many sold

Later we cycled home together and the city was transformed. The stars let out a kaleidoscopic light. The night sky embraced us in indigo hues. The light from the houses beckoned us homeward and the sweet scented autumn air kissed us gently.

There was no way I was going to let her leave me at the gate even though the guard gave us an odd look and said, 'You must be out by eleven,' gruffly.

'Isn't there anyway out except through the gates I ask ?'

'Not unless you jump from the first floor balcony.'

'I think the Italians are best at that. We Chinese are happy if there enough time for tea.

'There's just enough time for that'

Luckily her roommate hasn't appeared yet and I have the chance to invite her out the following Saturday. I am so anxious she will say no but she agrees.

'But you must go or you will be in trouble' and she urges me out the door.

I know she is right.

But my heart is light.

Lighter than a seagull's.

Chapter 6: Romance in the Muslim Quarter.

I woke up the next morning in a panic; thinking I'm scared, scared, really scared. Am I just a fool again an **eejit;** opening up to that world of feeling that dark ocean that could sink or swim me. Could it be the void; are there great black holes in human relationships just like there are great black holes in the universe. Does negativity draw us in like gravity does the stars into the void?

As I begin to dress myself and go wash in the bathroom I am contemplating the language we use when we fall in love. I'm crazy about you. Am I going crazy? The happy madness of it, the wanting to see you the needing to be with you that everything else takes on the feel of you. They say you'll recognise the man of your dreams from his eyes. I'll bring those eyes with me to the afterlife…….

My reverie was interrupted by the knock on the door of the courtyard. I realised the person had been knocking for quite some time. It was Qi on his bike. My heart effervesced with delight and excitement as I managed to invite him inside in a calm voice. I directed him to one of the two armchairs in the room and he sat looking so composed with a faintly smiling face. I asked him, secure in the cloak of custom, if he would like some tea. He did not give the customary response; instead he inquired inquisitively what brand of tea I had.

'*Dragon well,*' I replied, 'but why do you ask?'

Oh because names in Chinese are often portents for the future and *Dragon well* this is a very good sign for a new beginning. In that moment our eyes locked in a knowing stare, not wanting to leave each other's vision. And we gazed at each other in the hungry stare of first love, feasting on the wonder of each other for the first time. As the light flowing from the courtyard through the living room window caught his face he appeared to me the most handsome man I had ever seen. His golden brown skin framed his amber eyes, which were set above high chiselled cheekbones and a smooth nose. He had about him the serenity of a Buddha with a playful enthusiasm for life.

I poured the boiled water from the flask onto the Dragon well tea in the cups dragging my eyes away from him. Then I noticed he was searching in his bag for something. Out came his hand and he threw an object in the air between us to catch. I grabbed it with one free hand and saw it was a rag doll. It took me a split second to understand the symbolism of the gesture from the film *Red Sorghum* where the girl threw the doll at the boy she liked. I think I must have blushed because he laughed,

'Just one of the many gifts I will give to you.'

'Thank you, it's lovely,' I replied as I played with it to relieve my nervous tension and shyness.

Chi by contrast seemed so cool and at ease as he sipped his tea and said 'Your tea is very powerful I think it is increasing my attraction to you.'

'Well you can blame the Chinese manufacturer for that.'

'I am not blaming anyone I am very grateful.'

'I only hope I am not relying on it for my attractiveness.'

'Have no fear I could swim in those jade eyes of yours for an eternity and only feel bliss.'

'Be careful then that you don't drown in them.

Oh what a wonderful way to die but lets not talk about death in a time when it's so good to be alive. There's so much I want to show and do with you. Have you ever been to the Muslim quarter?'

'Well I've only been living here three months and the Muslim quarter is hardly a secret.'

'Ah but I mean the old Muslim quarter within the quarter.'

'Is this some kind of Chinese riddle?'

'Not quite. I'm talking about the heart of the Muslim centre where only the Uigur care to thread and the Han population leave them largely to themselves.'

'Can't say that I do or I don't. I guess I'll find out when I get there. Let's get on our bikes.'

'On our bikes,' he repeated after me taking off my Irish lilt.

They wheeled like the rest of the inhabitants along the broad bicycle lanes that circumscribed the expansive boulevards of the city. Eventually they came to the old part of the town where the streets narrowed and curled and they had to vie with motorised vehicles and pedestrians for precious space. Here the old Chinese courtyards with their wooden balconies, arched doorways and triangular tiled red roofs had not yet become the victims of modernisation. The streets were now cobblestone and pedestrianised so they parked up at a bicycle lot and received a receipt from a burly uniformed bicycle attendant who sported a knowing grin.

'Does that look on his face mean we have official approval,' Kayleigh asked?'

'Must be a really auspicious day' Chi smiled. 'Actually the authorities have relaxed considerably about relations with foreigners. Of course we are not allowed to sleep in the same room but neither is a Chinese couple who aren't married.'

'Not that that is an immediate concern.' she quipped.

'Of course not,' he laughed, 'considering the intellectual nature of our relationship.'

A green and sporting Arabic calligraphy marked the main food market street. It was lined with poky little dumpling shops as well as full size quality restaurants. On the pavements were rows of street stalls selling noodles and stews from steaming cauldrons, spiced mutton basting on skewers, varieties of nuts and seeds on metal plates, and boiled sweets and coconut based brightly coloured desserts. On the right hand side was a large Mosque, which incorporated Arabic features into a familiar Chinese design. Through the stone archway marking its entrance there was a courtyard with a minaret, in the shape of a Pagoda.

As they pressed through the milling crowd, Chi caught her

hand in his and a delighted warm vibration shot from her hand to her heart and nestled there contentedly as though it had found its final resting place. She looked at him furtively and was sure love radiated from her eyes despite her cautionary tone.

'Aren't you concerned that we will be seen?'

'It is not against the law in China to hold hands; many young people do nowadays.'

'But is it not viewed as another western decadence especially with a foreigner.'

'These attitudes are changing and besides I've always wanted to try it.

'You mean I am the privileged first one?'

'The first and only.'

'Isn't it a bit early to say?'

'No, not for something like true love which exists outside the limits of time.'

And as he looked deep into my eyes again I could feel this truth. I felt light and boundless and radiant with love. And looking at him I knew he felt the same way.

Chi's friend's arrival on the scene wasn't long grounding us. With their strong physical handshakes and their hearty voices they awaited us under the archway that marked the entrance of their restaurant. Wearing decorative round Muslim hats atop rounded ruddy faces that sported beards and whiskers they led us with their aprons to the open courtyard where a feast was already half waiting on a long timber table.

Centre of the table a gas flame boiled a bubbling stew of mutton. Circling the pot were plates filled with meat, salad, bread and an assortment of spice vinegar and nut sauces. The exotic spells wafted up the nasal passages and set the taste buds dancing.

A train of singers in a dazzling assortment of coloured cottons echoed the choral melodies of the herd's people from the grasslands as they galloped across the plains. The first singer carried a Hada (a cloth woven of blue, red and yellow thread) between his outstretched hands and handed it to the eldest guest; a grey bearded Muslim man. The second singer offered a drink of white wine alcohol from a silver tray full of eggcup size glasses. The singing continues while all ten guests are served in this way and then we settle into the divine food. Meanwhile the hosts fill our bowls with beer and replenish them after almost every sip so that it becomes impossible to keep track of what you are drinking.

I whisper to Chi, 'obviously different rules govern alcohol consumption for Muslim's in China.'

The older Muslims are often quite strict but since hashish is often in short supply the younger ones often relax with alcohol. Our conversation is interrupted by the loud noises of the two men arguing opposite in Chinese. One is Tibetan and the other Uigur but because their Chinese is not native as a companion non native speaker I can understand them more easily.

'Hu Yao Beng has strong support within the party. Under his influence political reform will follow economic reform. Soon there will be more freedom for Muslims and Tibetans in China thanks to Hua Yao Bong.'

It's the old Tibetan Gaytso with the heavily furrowed dark brow of centuries of knowledge who is speaking. With gusto he raises up off his chair and shouts, 'three cheers for freedom!' He looks a majestic sight, a tall slim man of noble bearing with his grey fur hat and his long black cloak rimmed in white fur and tied with a red sash. The others rise in unity but in the subsequent hush a rotund Muslim man, Guo Le, in a white skull cap and blue Mao suit draws the group's attention by his equally commanding presence.

'I wish I could share your optimism for the sake of all minority groups in China. But you must remember Huo Yao Beng is not the party leader and his views are not shared by Deng Xiao Peng. Peng wants economic reform but not political reform. The Communist party do not want China to break up like the former Soviet Union.'

'Maybe you are right,' says Gaytso 'but all I am saying is that now is the time to push for political reform within the current system. More control over Tibetans by Tibetans and the same for Muslims and to stop the huge influx of Han Chinese to these regions.'

'As long as the Han Chinese need more space they'll continue to be plant Han Chinese in minority areas says Chi. Tibet and Xinjiang are too important militarily politically and economically for the Chinese to return them back to the minorities. Xinjiang borders the Muslim Soviet provinces of Uzbekistan and Tajikistan. And there is a real risk of them uniting with their Muslim brotherhood in those countries. As for Tibet it acts as a buffer zone between India and China. Its huge resources and area make it too valuable to concede.'

'But surely,' says Gaytso 'economic reform will have some effect on the political system after all if the Government is prepared to release some control over the economy this affects its power of taxation and distribution of goods and services, the nature of state employment etc.'

'Yes but whether this would lead to a multi party system and to increased autonomy for the minorities is another issue says Chi. In the final analysis the future of the country is very dependant on whom the army gives its allegiance to; those in favour of economic reform only led by Deng Xiao Peng, those in favour of political and economic reform led by Hu Yao Beng or the reactionary elements, the old die hard communists who want neither.'

'And which one do you think will succeed teacher Chi?' asks Guo Le, the Muslim.

'Who I think will succeed and who I'd like to see succeed unfortunately are not the same. I think Deng has control within the politburo and perhaps the support of most of the people though in China since we do not have opinion polls it's difficult to tell. After all the reforms are bringing prosperity for the entrepreneurs and the farmers. Hu Yao Beng has only minor support within the bureau and among the masses but he has a lot of support from the intellectuals and students. The vast majority of Chinese the peasants and the workers do not know what democracy is never mind voting for it. Democracy requires education and at the very least literacy which in our language is difficult to attain. As for the minorities the majority of the Han people adopt the party line and don't even consider the rights of the ethnic groups.'

'Sounds very fatalistic.' Chi I butted in

'Not fatalistic dear one but realistic. But then who am I to predict the future. A wise man would never do that and I am definitely not wise.'

'Lets drink to our foolish friend.' says Gaytso.

'Long may his folly reign! Dry glass.'

'Gan bei dry glass!' everyone rejoined in Chinese.

'And to his lovely companion and our foreign friend Kayleigh may they have a long and happy future together. Perhaps in the future you can let the world know what is happening to the minorities in the provinces' says Guo Le.

Then Chi stood up to raise his glass and said; 'and to our hospitable hosts and charming friends Guo Le and Gaytso long life and double happiness' and he raised his glass of bai jui

As everyone cheered *gan bei* he whispered to me; 'it would be appropriate for you to give thanks now also.'

'Oh!' I said very flushed, standing up and swaying after the devilish white spirit.

'I am overwhelmed by your kindness and hospitality the succulence of your food and the sparkle from your drink and most of all the humour and charm of your company. The thing that amazes me about you and your leaders in particular the Dalai Lama is you complete lack of bitterness towards the Chinese. Your attitude of forgiveness is a bright light to all people in conflict. I'd like to raise a toast to the minority people of China, to your freedom and compassion.Gan bei!' I say,' as I all but flop into the chair.'

They pulled away the tables and the music started and

before I knew it I was being whirled along from spin to spin to the strains of an Arabian night of sitars flutes and drums and Mata Hare.

Chapter 7: Triangle

'Tra la la la la triangle' goes the country and western song and if the course of true love rarely runs smooth it appears in China to meander and twist, divert and even at times be dammed by the intervention of third parties.

In that labyrinth of whispers, gossip and underground information, the human connection of curiosity that interlinks us all word of Chi and Kayleigh's rendezvous was nearly out before they met.

Of course it could have been Ming or anyone of the myriad people at the exhibition. But all of the signs pointed to Fang Yuan. He was not to be outdone by anyone lest of all one of his friends. He'd had his eye on Kayleigh from the start even though he had been rather crude in expressing it. On her first day teaching his class he'd asked her what was a French letter. Kayleigh had dismissed this as an innocent linguistic curiosity, the expression on his face was so serious he couldn't have possibly have known its true meaning. She replied in totally even tone that it was a love letter and since no one in the room seemed embarrassed she decided neither was she. It was only later when she divulged with Julie who expressed disbelief at his innocence that she began to have her doubts.

'That fellow has been to Australia you know, sheep farming no less. I have him in my listening class. He appears older and wiser to me.'

Some weeks later he invited the two of them to dinner but this in itself did not alert her as it was customary for students as a courtesy to a foreign teacher to entertain them in their homes. Moreover, they were actually invited to a friend of his house along with Ming Wei so it all appeared very innocuous at first. That night however Fang Yuan was obviously using

Ming Wei as a conduit to illicit personal information about the two of them. Looking back at the ploy it was quite comical in its stumbling attempt at deviousness.

Fang's friend's name was Do Han Toe and he welcomed them at the door. He was a tall handsome man by any standards with refined features and a well-proportioned face. His pale skin lent him an air of delicacy though there was a wildness in his eyes that was reflected in his untidy dress, unusual for a Chinese, he wore an oversize T-shirt with jeans. He bore a comical smile on his face as if he thought their attempts at Chinese were amusing or they themselves were amusing to look at.

For this reason Kayleigh didn't feel cheeky asking him why he had shaved his head.

He said because he was going away on a business trip.

She asked Fang Yuan why he would have to shave his head to go on a trip.

The two of them looked at each other amused and talked in a Chinese local dialect she couldn't understand.

And then Fang Yuan looked her in the eye and said;

'He shaved his head for his wife.'

'But why did he shave his head for his wife?' asks Julie, starting to get interested.

'To prove to her that he will not be with another woman when he goes away.'

'And does his wife think that will stop him?'

He translated what she said to Doe Han Toe.

Doe Han Toe laughs and says in Chinese, 'Would one of them go out with me looking like this?'

They laughed but they could see his wife, Zhu Hua, had a worried look on her face so both Julie and Kayleigh said no, in Chinese and added firmly;

'We wouldn't go with a married man anyway. It is considered wrong in our society too.'

'Anyway he looks like a monk, doesn't he Julie?' Kayleigh covered her laughter with her right hand.

Julie cracked up again.

'What did they say, what did they say? asks Do Han Toe.

Fang Yuan translates for him.

And he laughs another big hearty laugh and turns to Zhu Hua and says; 'Now don't you believe me?'

The look Zhu Hua gives shows she is not convinced and she says she must return to Ming Wei in the kitchen. As they sit at the glass table in the pale green room sipping tea and chewing seeds and apples the girls learn more about the two men. Drinking beer they were in revelatory mood and divulge a lot about themselves. They had been friends since childhood in the sixties and were typical of the new Chinese mind that doesn't believe in religion, propaganda or party. They didn't like the restrictions imposed on them by the state and weren't afraid to say so to foreigners any way.

'But;' says Fang Yuan, explaining to them in English, 'you have to be cautious with other Chinese unless you know them well. Since the Cultural Revolution few people feel safe to talk freely. So many people were spied on by others. We know of a lot of people who had been treated badly, either beaten or killed or sent to labour camps.'

There was a wildness about those two men that Kayleigh hadn't witnessed before in other Chinese; a restlessness, an energy that was hyper, they were fidgety, sinewy and carried no extra flesh.

Suddenly Fang Yuan jumps up and pops into the kitchen and over the sounds of the sizzling stir fry they can hear him instruct Ming Wei in Chinese;

'Find out their personal details'

Ming Wei emerged from the heat of the kitchen hot and flustered.

'Zhu Hua wants to know what age you are.'

Julie replied, suppressing her surprise at the bluntness of the question, 'You can look at our CVs in Mr Wang's office.'

Ming Wei retreated to the kitchen with the correct ages, which they could hear because she had to shout over the sound of frying. Then some more heated hurried whispers and she emerged again with;

'Do you have boyfriends?

They answered a resounding yes.

Back in again went Ming Wei with the answer and out again with another question;

'Are you engaged to be married?'

This also had to be translated and they both answered no.

And so the evening continued with a long trail of questions about their likes and dislikes and beliefs until the food was ready.

As they were eating Do Han Toe's only son Xin popped in the door but hid behind his mother's legs when he saw the foreigners. They persuaded him to give a karate demonstration. He was very agile and adroit and not shy of performing.

'He is only seven', said his Dad, obviously proud of his ability. Physical strength counted a lot in a land of slight built people it seemed.

The rest of the evening was an attempt by Fang Yuan to unwind them both with Mao-Tai and beer and trying to divulge more personal information from them. Kayleigh thought it all quite amusing and was happy to stay but Julie gave the visual signal for her to leave.

On the cycle home Julie uncharacteristically let the anger erupt.

'Well I never, that Fang Yuan is just beyond belief like a bloody interview with a vampire. The cheek, he was trying to assess us for marriage prospects!'

'I don't think so.'

'Why the forty questions?'

'Curiosity?'

'No no there was far more to it than that. But what was he up to? Is he really interested in the two of us as prospects or was one of us the stool pigeon? But then again is he delicate enough for that? I found the whole thing too embarrassing'

'I thought it was just a laugh.'

'You would.'

'Really no harm can come of it, it's not as if we are forced into bondage and whipped off as slave brides.'

'But he's our student for goodness sake; actually mine and I have to face him tomorrow. It's highly irregular if not out of bounds.'

'Just pretend like it never happened. You were pretty adamant about your loyalties to Robert anyway.'

Looking back on it later Kayleigh realised she had been quite attracted to Yuan in a visceral way. There was something about him that smelt of an animal on the hunt and contrary to her intellect she found him exciting to be around. She usually felt a rise in temperature in his presence. Had the strain of having to control this added to her excitement? He too seemed to be under constant strain in her presence. She herself reasoned that he operated under such tension all the time. As if he was constantly hiding something. What was he thinking? she wondered. She figured however that his eyes didn't lie whatever about the erect spine and the tightened movement of the hands. There was softness in his eyes that he obviously thought was hidden by the frame of his glasses and so in this respect he had left down his guard and he showed affection. It was for this reason she was kind to him or was it because deep down she also had a deep affection for him. He was after all great for a joke and she could relax with him. But she didn't like the way he connived with Ming Wei to deter her forming a relationship with Chi. Shortly after her trip to the Muslim quarter with Chi the two came to her rooms. Her suspicions were aroused as they did not normally associate together and being of opposite sex it was not proper etiquette in Chinese society for them to be seen as a pair on their own.

'May we come in' says Ming in her formal tones.

'We have something important to tell you.' Her black eyes had an intense gaze that seared through a person, making them feel that they had been shot through by something as accurate and cold as a steel pellet.

'Fang Yuan he speak sincerely' begins Ming.

Kayleigh didn't like the intense atmosphere created by the presence of the devious duo and sought to dispel it by adding a light-hearted tone.

'Gosh what can be so serious that you won't sit down and have a cup of tea?'

But they are a determined train.

'No thank you.' they say in unison

But Kayleigh is determined also.

'I'll take that as a Chinese *no* meaning *yes*.

She pours some of the ubiquitous Chinese green tea and entreats them to sit down.

'Miss Kayleigh I hear Chi Hai O is keeping the company with you,' says Fang, not touching his tea. 'You see in our Chila the news travels very fast and this reason alone for you to take care. In addition we must warn you even though I am the good friend of him'.

'Do you mind if I smoke,' he lit up in a fidgety way and seemed unusually tense. Beside him Ming was her usual rigid self but in this atmosphere she looked even more severe than ever - like a stern schoolmistress about to give a lecture to one of her students. There didn't seem to be much kindness in her heart. Kayleigh wondered did she miss her daughter all the way back in Xinjiang or did she blame her daughter for losing her husband. Ming Wei had told Kayleigh that her husband had left her because she had a girl and not a boy. Was she really a spy like some of the students suggested, but why and to what gain? And Fang who gave away nothing with his looks what was he really feeling? Did that inscrutable face represent a real lack of emotion or was he trying hard to conceal a real feeling. She'd rather think it was the later. It was rumoured that his family suffered a lot during the Cultural Revolution and he was separated from them and adopted by his present parents. He was very dark and elemental and something in his darkness seduced her but she instinctively knew she could never really trust him.

Today she could feel the tension in the air like a Tai chi sword suspended between them.

'I am a good friend of Chi' he continued. 'I've known him since boyhood. I must to warn you for your own sake. Chi is a brilliant artist everyone in our *Chila* we know that but is very difficult for an artist to make a living in *Chila.* Most of the time they must teach and have no time to paint.

Only a very few artists officially recognised make a living from their work. Chi's style of art is not official style. He has many Western influences even democratic some say – making a political statement.

It's much better for Chi to go to abroad. You are understanding my point.'

Before he has time to pause Ming rounds off the assault.

'What Fang Yuan says is correct. Many Chinese men like this, even *married* will marry again to go abroad.'

'You have a very poor opinion of Chinese men and especially Chi,' says Kayleigh trying to float above their intensity by circling around them pouring tea and dishing out biscuits and melon seeds.

'But it's true it's true,' says Ming as if she is talking from her own experience.

'Many of students here think you came here to get married because you are old by Chinese standard and should be married already so they think you easy target.'

Although Kayleigh realises Ming has a different cultural perspective in that most Chinese feel obligated by their culture to get married and quite young she finds it difficult not to be offended. She calmly reassures Ming that with women's liberation in the West some women choose to marry late if not at all.

'But why are you interested in Chi,' asks Duan, 'when I on the other hand am so sincere in my intentions. With my connections in Australia I can go to abroad anytime. My interest is only in you.'

Kayleigh is in no way convinced by Fang Yuan and her patience is beginning to wear thin.

'Thank you for your declaration Fang. It is most flattering and thank you both for your concern but I have class in ten minutes and I must go.' With the teapot still in her hand she ushers them to the door.

'And please don't worry about me. As you say I am an old woman by Chinese standards so I should be able to take care of myself.'

And she closes the door firmly on them. As soon as she is sure they have gone, their footfall echoing on the stairs, she sits down, cupping her eyes with her hands and lets the tears flow with relief, exhaustion, and confusion. Who could she believe? Who could she turn to? For the first time she felt the trickle of doubt about Chi. The trickle that turned into a stream of tears. A flood to wash the fears of the heart.

So when Chi phoned that evening he was stunned by the cold reception. She said she needed time to think. Things were going a little too fast. But Chi was suspicious and not easily deterred.

'Someone has been talking to you. I know enough about our Chila to know this. Who was it someone from the Foreign Affairs or the English department?'

'Sorry Chi I am too upset to talk now. I just need some time.'

'Ok. I understand. Just you take the good care of your self for now. I will find out what is going on.'

Meanwhile Kayleigh wrote to Molly.

Do you really think Chi could be that conniving? He seems so sincere and patriotic. He never talks about leaving China. I think he is genuinely interested in improving conditions here.

And Molly replies,

From what you have written previously Chi does seem very sincere and Fang Yuan appears to be the devious one. Of course we always have to keep at the back of our mind that a Chinese man may be trying to escape to the West but in this case it would appear it's just a matter of plain jealousy on Fang Yuan's part. I wish I could come for the Harvest Moon Festival but the break is very short for travelling such a long distance and my students want me to celebrate with them. Kayleigh resolved not to think about Chi again until her mind was clear and her heart calm. But her resolve did not last long. The Chinese folk music he'd given her reminded her of him. Everything reminded her of him; the green tea in the morning, the distinctive lemon of the Chinese Autumn light, his face in the face of her students, his footsteps falling in every footstep on her stairs, his hand offering the bowl of steaming beef noodles from the college cauldron, his back bent over every bicycle on her way, his voice in every Chinese word sung, his whisper in the darkness of night. The memories, oh, the memories, she thought, the past making connections to every pattern of the present. Sometimes she felt that love itself can exist more in absence than in presence. His absence swelled up in her until all she could feel was his presence in every pore of her skin, in every cell of her body, in every awareness of consciousness. And with this came the realisation that Chi was everything Fang wasn't. He was truth, he was love, he was a bright light from above.

Her discussion with Julie resolved her doubts.

'How could you be so daft?' Says Julie with an incredulous look on her face. 'I never trusted that Fang Yuan since that ridiculous match making dinner. Of course Ming Wei went along because she couldn't bear anyone to be happy since she's so miserable herself. It's rather obvious to me who the real gold digger is.'

'I suppose I was just so scared of being hurt again,' confided Kayleigh.

'Well of course there are no guarantees in love but at the very least you have a good chance with Chi.'

Still she did not see or hear from him again until the harvest moon festival two weeks later.

As it turned out the party was held at Fang Yuan's parents

house while they were away. It was a typical old Chinese courtyard; cobblestone with a central flowerbed of hollyhocks. It was particularly lovely that night as the traditional Chinese lanterns lit it up. A twinkling light danced as the glow from each red lantern jumped to the next, kissing romance into the hearts of the guests as they joined the intimate setting. Favourite Chinese folk music emanated from a tape recorder on a table. There were at least forty people there between students and teachers. Some were standing chatting around tables laden with moon cakes, dried fruit, seeds, beer and soft drinks. Others were already enchanted by the atmosphere of the evening and the bright moon that streamed through the courtyard and were dancing western style waltzes to the music.

Fang Yuan was waiting at the courtyard door as Kayleigh and Julie made their entrance. He greeted them both warmly and straight away led Kayleigh to Chi. Poor Kayleigh nearly passed out on the spot when she saw him. He was even more gorgeous than when she remembered and he had such a captivating spell over her with his presence alone. He's never going to forgive me for doubting him she thought.

'I was just explaining to Chi about our misunderstanding,' says Fang Yuan at pains to make amends. 'I think it was just my poor English. You know Chi and I are such good friends I would never say anything to hurt him. Ming and I were just trying to protect you and Chi understands that perfectly. So sorry for any misunderstanding.'

'It's alright Fang Yuan, all is forgiven,' says Chi with a laugh. 'Come on Kayleigh lets dance.'

As he led her out to the court yard Kayleigh felt the comfort of his steady arms in the soothing rhythm of his gentle sway and whispered softly in her ear, 'don't worry about Fang I think he does really like you so he tried his best to come between us. What is it you say in the west again; all's fair in love and war?'

'Still Chi, you are good friends.'

'I know but do not worry about it now after all he did bring us back together again.'

With that they let the words give way to the sway of the music.

Some time later when she was relieved that she was keeping rhythm with him Kayleigh whispered;

'I never realised you were such a good dancer.'

'Just as well he laughed since you don't seem to know how to waltz at all.'

'Sorry Chi but waltzing is not popular among young people in the west,' she says as she deliberately stamped on his toe.

'Ai ya!' he cried as he grabbed her more tightly and sent her spinning and laughing into the red lantern lit night.

Chapter 8: Time for Tibet

They had decided to go to Taersi, the most important Buddhist monastery outside the current politically recognised Tibet, for the weekend. Actually it was Fang Yuan's idea as he was trying to redeem himself after his deplorable behaviour. He was a driver after all and could get a jeep for free under the rules of the danwei (work unit); a wonderful advantage in a country where individual ownership of cars was not allowed at the time. The jeep itself was a wonder of Chinese engineering a big solid square green bulk in military style, a throwback to the Second World War. Despite the kangaroo suspension it was a comfortable enough ride. Fang Yuan and Doe Han Toe would share the driving and Julie, Kayleigh and Chi were stuffed in the back with the provisions for the road, a flask of tea, some beer, boiled eggs, mian bao (steamed bread), fruit and seeds. As they made their way from the city to the countryside the landscape became less and less peopled, the road rougher and they started to be swallowed up by the undulating landscape of plains and mountains. The elegant mountains sported prayer wheels and the verdant grasslands were strewn with wild flowers where semi nomadic horseman rode with herds of sheep and yak. So green more green than Ireland even, thought Kayleigh. They seemed to be rising higher into a broader plateau with sharper mountains in the background; still very green but getting cooler and the air more rarefied. Until less and less they encountered any traffic or human settlements. The few they did see were mud walled groups of houses and small villages with the occasional dab of whitewash to give some colour. Kayleigh and Julie pointed to the children playing in the laneways and the odd dog or two hanging about what seemed to be a well in the middle of a settlement. At Julie and

Kayleigh's suggestion they decided to stop to break the journey at the site of a prayer wheel on a steep mountain top. It was worth the trek though it did strain the breathing and the thigh muscles.

'Gosh I'm not as fit as I thought,' says Kayleigh out of breath. 'After all the cycling I do everyday.'

The Tibetan air can catch anyone, says Chi, you forget how high up we are.

It doesn't help that all the *Chinese* mountains have steps going up them. It makes one more lazy, quips Julie. Thank goodness we are near the top.

What a spectacular view! No wonder they mark them with these colourful flags it seems only right says Kayleigh.

Gosh says Julie what's that over there!

It's a bunch of large birds but what are they doing? cried Kayleigh.

It's the eagles feasting on the bodies of the dead, replied Chi. The Tibetans believe that their souls will be carried to heaven more quickly by the eagles.

Don't go too close says Duan they might get vicious.

After such a spectacular site they returned mutely down the mountain to the jeep. They passed through the last major town of Xining en route. It was still largely Chinese occupied, fed by the railway; part of the plantation of the Chinese Han population into the vastness of Tibet with its great reserves of oil coal and gas. They were still silently contemplative when they stopped at Huang Zhong the closest town to the monastery. At one of the many Muslim restaurants they supped on a hot bowl of noodles and vegetables as they watched with fascination the trading on the street. All manner of goods both dead and alive were being sold out of the backs of carts from poultry to wool to vegetables to hardware and clothing. There was a lot of very good natured haggling over price with everyone seeming genuinely satisfied.

What a variety of people says Kayleigh its lovely to see different tribes of Tibetan and Muslims buying and selling side by side.

The Muslim men wore white skull caps and the typical blue Mao suit of the Han Chinese whereas the women wore veils of different colours and materials. The Tibetans wore an assorted array of dress. Some men wore cowboy hats and big boots with large black wool coats. It was their coats that really fascinated the girls; they were more like cloaks than coats they were so voluminous; they were folded tent shape across the midriff and tied by a red sash. They were dark woollen brown and black outside and underneath lined with white fur. Then another group of men appeared obviously from a different tribe; wearing brightly coloured embroidered hats and fawn coats. The women also wore a variety of colourful headdress and plaited their hair in ornate fashion. Gold and silver decorated their neck and limbs and shawls, scarves and aprons added to their adornment. The Tibetans were taller than the Han or Muslim Chinese and so they stood out. They were ruddier in complexion too, not as clean or neat looking. They had a different stance, a different walk, a different outlook on life, freer in movement, more agile, less self conscious, carrying with them the mountain air, the taste of freedom and the wildness of the west.

One couple in particular delighted Kayleigh and Julie with their colour, joviality and unity. He wore a cowboy hat garnished with feathers and a colourful bandana; the woman wore a red scarf and a double braid down her back she had a cheerful ruddish countenance with a huge smile that erupted whit embarrassment when she saw Julie and Kayleigh looking at her. They felt empathy with her a foreigner too but in her own land. Chi was sitting back smiling to himself enjoying the spectacle but Doe and Fang Yuan were observing coolly, clearly not amused and it seemed like a glass pane shut down between them and the girls. But the girls were too intrigued by the couple to pull back and asked if they could take photos showing their cameras. Julie had an extensive background in photography and had even set up her own dark room in the bathroom. She had encouraged Kayleigh to buy a Nikon SLR lens in Hong Kong to get close up and personal encounters with her subjects. It was a revelation the world it opened up to her but she was happier in automatic mode than making manual adjustments like the professional Julie was. The couple wanted to have a look at the instruments and examined them with the curiosity of children. A crowd was beginning to gather so they started to move quickly with the photography, close ups on hands, faces, details of costume. They asked them if they had any photos of the Dalai Lama with a deep knowingness in their eyes. Kayleigh said, I'm sorry we don't.

At this stage they were becoming an ever widening spectacle so they said goodbye and moved back inside to the relative privacy of the restaurant where Chi commended them for their determination but the two others gave them rather frosty looks. They paid the bill and headed out. Fang Yuan and Doe had already decided they were staying at the hotel just outside the monastery as they said they were not really interested in *religious ideology* as they called it. Kayleigh got the impression they were uncomfortable outside their own tribe. They all agreed to meet up the next day for lunch. As the three approached the monastery on foot, rucksacks on backs, they could see that it consisted of a large complex of colourful buildings set spectacularly in the cleft of a valley. The entrance to the monastery was dramatically set by a row of eight stupas, bulbous shaped structures with gilded heads. They bought a single ticket to visit the monastery and a young monk in dusty burgundy robes and huge leather boots offered to give them a guided tour for twenty Yuan. He spoke English with an American accent and Kayleigh asked him where he had learnt it.

An American student came here to do his Masters degree on Tibetan Buddhism and he taught me and a number of others in exchange for his accommodation.

'Seems like he did an excellent job.' says Kayleigh.

'Thank you,' he said with a broad smile.

Immediately they entered the monastery walls an air of gentle tranquillity descended upon them, not a shroud of solemnity or a cloak of heaviness but a lightness, a freshness, a certain joviality. There were children playing and laughing in the courtyards. Many of the monks were languishing happily in the doorways of the temples whilst some went about their daily chores of carrying water and food and collecting wood. Most of the pilgrims wore an easy smile as if it were just a customary part of their facial expression. They ambled around the monastery with an ease and comfort that would relax even the most tense of visitors.

We were wondering if there are any rooms available in the monastery at the moment, asked Chi with a mischievous hint of a Yankee accent.

The monastery hotel has several rooms and cheap, the monk smiled, detecting the play on his accent. Let me take you there and you can unburden yourselves of your bags. He guided them to a two storey wooden building brightly painted in reds, blues and yellows though the paint was peeling and the stairs up to the balcony floor was rickety.

In the centre of the bed room was the traditional stove for lighting coal shaped in thick rings for that purpose. The beds were wooden, painted brightly and the walls were decorated with flowers and Buddhas.

Chi turned to the two girls; 'well, what do you think?'

'I think its charming,' said Kayleigh

'Lets take it,' said Julie and they bought flopped to the bed with their mini rucksacks

'Your room is down the hall,' said the monk to Chi with a knowing smile. 'I will show you.'

'I guessed that,' Chi replied again in American tone.

'We will come back and have some Chinese tea with you here if it pleases you,' the monk turned to the girls and then they left.

The girls collapsed in giggles on the bed as soon as they were out of earshot.

'You can have some Chinese tea if it pleases you, where did he get that phrase; sounds really post colonial rather than American.'

'And I thought in a monastery at least we'd get to try the local tea with yak butter,' says Julie.

Maybe it's just as well says Kayleigh I think it might be a bit early in the day for me, that yak butter smells very strong and its odour is all over the place from the candles.

Perhaps you are right.

When they returned with the tea flask and cups Julie asked Tsering to tell them a little about the monastery.

The monastery was built in 1560 in honour of Tsongkhapa the founder of The Yellow Hat or Gelupa sect of Tibetan Buddhism. It is also the former home of the Dalai Lama who is the leader of the Yellow Sect. Pilgrims come from all over Tibet Mongolia and China to visit here. Yellow sect Buddhism is only one of the many forms of Buddhism in Tibet and of course it has been influenced by the native Bon religion which was animist, believing that all things have life or a soul.

A lot of early religions around the world believed that says Kayleigh.

So do little children, they see life in a stone, says Julie

I suppose the modern scientific notion of Gaia also conforms to believing the earth is a living organism says Kayleigh.

They finished their tea and followed Tsering to the stupas at the entrance to begin their tour. As they stood to marvel at the monuments Julie asked Tsering why they were built.

They originated from the Indian word *stupa,* which was a funeral monument. Here in Tibet they are called chortens which means a receptacle for offerings. Not all chortens are tombs although some do contain ashes or corpses of holy men others may hold important Buddhist relics.

Is that what the little doors are for asks Kayleigh

Yes says Tsering but the chorten also has special symbolic

significance for us Buddhists; the spire is made of thirteen parasols, which represents the number of steps towards enlightenment. The four steps below the bulb represent the stages of learning.

They are so beautifully painted as well. Where do you get your paints? asks Chi

Many are naturally dyes, but in modern times we are also importing from China

Do you mind if we take some photos? asks Julie.

Not outside here but there are some sacred places inside where it may not be permitted but you will see the signs.

What about the people asks Kayleigh do they mind you taking their photos?

Mostly no but some people are shy of course but with that special telescope lens of yours many people cannot tell can they?

No but generally I can sense if they are comfortable or relaxed.

At the Big Tile Hall they listened to monks praying. They sat cross legged in their burgundy robes some in their yellow peaked hats of the Gelupa sect, many with wooden beads in their hands chanting their way into a semi trance like state it seemed to Kayleigh. And she thought and I shall have some peace there because peace comes dropping slow and at that moment she felt very united with Chi and Julie and the monks and the pulsating vibration of the prayers as they shook the great hall.

Eventually they got uncomfortable sitting cross-legged and made whispers to Tsering that they needed to move on. They entered the Hall of the Butter Sculptures. Here events in the Buddhas life were represented by sculptures made out of yak butter and brightly painted. They made some offerings of flowers and fruit to the great big golden Buddha.

Different Buddhas represent the stages of his life; the thin serious one is the early Buddha, the fat jolly one is the older Buddha, explained Tsering.

Outside they saw the monks debating. It was a sporty spectacle as they were standing facing each other in two lines and gesticulating dramatically with their hands and bodies.

That afternoon the three of them went off unguided on the pilgrim path. Along the dusty trail and above and beyond the monastery itself they followed in the footsteps of family or individual pilgrims as they kowtowed their way ahead. This kowtow involved an elaborate sequence of movements whereby the pilgrim lay face flat down on the ground raised themselves to their elbows in press up position and then up onto their knees and into a walking position until the next kowtow not much further on. Their whole bodies got covered in dust: face hands and hair. The children seemed to get great pleasure from this and the adults seemed to get gratification too. They encountered openings into the rocks where hermits lived; a flapping cover and a flag showing the only sign of human habitation.

They evening they were invited for a chat with the head of the monastery in his room. It was humble and simple and small but the hospitality was palpable in his warm smile and his soothing presence. He spoke in a soft voice interpreted by Tsering.

He asked then where they were from

When Kayleigh said she was from Ireland.

The Lama said that he heard the west of Ireland was a very spiritual place from other Tibetan monks who had been there.

Yes says Kayleigh we are mainly Catholic but there is a growing interest in Tibetan Buddhism there as well as other religions. There are even Tibetans Buddhist centre in Ireland now.

I think that is a good thing says the Lama. Acceptance and tolerance of different religions is vital, as the world has become such a small place. One religion cannot satisfy all people due to different cultures, state of mind etc. Probably is best to stay with one's original religion as it is more suited to ones culture and customs but that is up to the individual, the more people travel they more influences they will come under, the more they have the opportunity to compare and contrast different belief systems. But it is important to remember that there is a central unity in all religion and that is to teach about love, compassion and forgiveness. Too much emphasis is put on the differences between religions rather than their similarities. Every religion teaches the same message to be a warm hearted person. They all emphasise compassion and forgiveness

But what would be the main beliefs of Yellow sect Buddhism asks Julie. They were all seated cross-legged in a circle around the lama and it lent to the feeling of mutual exchange.

The lama responded in a soothing warm voice coming from his gentle countenance. We Buddhists believe that it is important for a person's mental state to always remain calm. Even if disturbances occur they should remain short and not affect your basic mental attitude. One can overcome the forces of negative emotions like anger and hatred by cultivating their counter forces like love and compassion. The practice of meditation helps to achieve calmness.. Buddhists also believe that most suffering in this life is caused by being overly attached to the things of this world whether that be another person, material possession or even life itself. Buddhists believe in the impermanence of things, that all things are in a state of change and therefore grasping onto things as if they were permanent can only create suffering. We must develop a certain level of detachment from the things of this world in order to keep our peace of mind. So Buddhist try to cultivate a state of mind known as cessation whereby all negative emotions and thoughts are eliminated. This is why the Buddha became an object of refuge not because Buddha was from the beginning a special person but because Buddha realised the state of true cessation.

But why do people get angry then asks Chi, what is its purpose?

The Lama smiled gently and replied. On the basis of compassionate motivation anger may in some cases be useful because it gives us extra energy and enables us to act swiftly. However anger usually leads to hatred and hatred is always negative. We can eliminate anger from our lives by cultivating a positive outlook on life and seeing the interconnectedness of all things. Even in the extreme case of an enemy if we look at it from another angle only an enemy gives us the opportunity to practice patience. No one else provides us with the opportunity for tolerance. Only those people we know who create problems for us provide us with the opportunity to practice tolerance and patience.

But what if your enemy does try to harm you as in the case of China and Tibet? asks Kayleigh.

You should act with wisdom and common sense without anger or hatred. Anger or hatred are blind and destructive whereas wisdom and common sense are clear and effective

For example in the case of Tibet we are following a non violent and compassionate way but this does not mean we should bow down and give in. we can try for a political and peaceful solution. The Dalai Lama advises us to harbour no hatred or anger towards our Chinese brothers and sisters who are harming us indeed the Dalai Lama has much sympathy with Marxist philosophy. Of course we must bring our people out of poverty. We do not want our women to be pulling ploughs or our children hungry, we do not want a return to the old feudal system. But under Chinese communism many people were killed, imprisoned, tortured or starved to death under the agricultural reforms. So we must continue to protect and sustain our own Tibetan people and culture in so far as we can. We Tibetans do not hold any hatred or bitterness towards the Chinese but just wish in a non violent way to get independence for Tibet. So even though the Dalai Lama was forced to flee Tibet in 1959 he still encourages people to visit to see the Tibetan way of life.

They said good bye and thanked Tsering and the Lama profusely and felt uplifted by the whole experience.

There is something about being on a mountain top that brings you closer to the mystery of your being sys Kayleigh.

There sure is said Chi, in his mock American accent. That night they slept very

peacefully in their monastery beds and woke to the early sounds of the monks

and chanting. They prayed with them in the monastery Hall of meditation and had

some yak tea with butter and bread for breakfast. They thanked them and bade farewell, knowing something fundamental inside them had changed. They rejoined Fang Yuan and Doe Han Toe at the hotel and made a tranquil journey back to Lanyuan.

Chapter 9: The Wedding

Even though we were a so-called love match the family insisted on doing our horoscopes as was the Chinese tradition. Luckily ours was an harmonious coupling; a monkey with a rat. Chi's father and sister Lily accompanied us to the family astrologer, an old Buddhist monk, in the nearby monastery.

'Very auspicious' he said in broken English, 'you two will be together long time. Very good relationship. I learnt the English from a missionary in the school but now very bad' and he reverts to Chinese. He gave us his blessing under the watchful gaze of the Buddha. We left our offerings of money and food at the Buddha's feet.

Under normal circumstances it was difficult for a Chinese person to marry a Westerner but more particularly Chi. He was an artist and the government did not want to lose his talent or commission from his work to the West. So there were bundles of red tape to go through. Chi came to my room one afternoon with a list of requirements from Foreign Affairs.

'I'm sorry to cause you so much trouble,' he said,' but this is our Communist bureaucracy, excuse me they have a lot of formalities, I wrote them down.

First, they need your passport, second, proof you aren't married before,

some official paper from your government. They also need some passport photos, a copy of your CV and references. I'm so sorry it's so much trouble.'

'Darling there is no need to apologise I'm sure it's a lot of paper work in my country too and for you of course it's worth it.

'I'm afraid that's not all. The application for marriage has to be processed by my Work Unit first and then head of the

Foreign Affairs Unit. Foreign Affairs will send a representative to interview you but don't worry just tell the truth you have nothing to hide. Have you? He smiled.

'Only three husbands ......but seriously Chi what are they looking for?'

'You know the policy change so often and depend on the individual too. Best thing be nice and friendly but serious and tell the truth because they may try to catch you out.'

A few days later I was summoned to the Department of Foreign Affairs Unit of the University by Huang Hu. I had had many transactions with her before about train tickets, travel permits, work cards and other administrative details. Although she was not the most senior official she was obviously chosen because she spoke English whereas the others spoke Russian. She had the typical Chinese accent often joked about by Westerners which was rendered more comical by the fact that she had a very extensive vocabulary and was very confident in her verbal ability. She had a pleasant round face which was enhanced by the intensity of her personality and the seriousness with which she performed her duty. On the desk in front of her she had a file into which she noted down my responses as she questioned me.

'Ah Kayleigh as you know it is responsibility Foreign Affairs Unit to do interview for you about your marriage. I do for you because this is normal procedure you understand for me. And I do for you a favour not make difficult for you. Now the first question; are you being married before?'

'No.'

'Are you sure?'

'Yes of course, I'm sure.'

'Ah so ah so.'

'But some students say you told them you married.'

'Oh that was a joke when they were trying to make a match for me '

'Oh I see,' and she eyed me intently, 'so no joking now, no married yes?'

'No not married Huang Hu.'

I had to take a few deep breaths to hide my amusement and exasperation.

'And the number two questions I have for you.'

'Why you want to marry Mr Chi Hai O?'

'Because we love each other.'

'Am sorry now Ms Kayla you do not take offence with me this not my question it's clear, Ministry ask this question. Mr Chi does not pay you to marry him to become an Irish citizen?'

'No no of course not. Chi is very happy in China and so am I we have not discussed living in Ireland.'

'Ok ok you understand this difficult for me too but must have to ask it my duty as Foreign affairs personal. So where you hope to live after marriage?'

'We were hoping to live at Chi's unit or mine.'

And as such the interview went on with no real surprise or difficulties except with exasperation with Huang Hu's English and effusive expression. After all that at the end of the interview she asked me to assist her with her application to a Foreign University. Of course I did not refuse which I'm sure helped to speed up the otherwise lengthy application process.

Meanwhile in my letters and phone calls home I tried to break the news gently to my family. In the early days these phone calls and letters were the umbilical cord that linked me to my family and my culture. They helped me to cope with the culture shock of the transition from Ireland to China; a transition I knew I had made when I started to dream in Chinese.

The most vivid of these dreams was played out underwater. I was playing volleyball with my Chinese students who slowly as the game went on turned into the members of my family and friends from primary school. However instead of talking in English they were speaking Chinese.

My first letters were full of the novelty of the new culture; the language lessons in Beijing, life from a bike, being on TV and then the letters about settling in Lanyuan.

My parent's letters by contrast were full of the weather and the happenings within the family and sadly as we all grow older news of those who passed away. My father was particularly encouraging because he had long had an avid interest in eastern culture and history. He was fascinated by the sound of the Chinese names the pronunciation of *Mousey Tongue* (Mao Ze Dong) especially amused him. The cultural achievements of the Chinese, in particular the Great Wall and the Xian Warriors also very much impressed him. His armchair travelled with me through these great places through my letters and I was constantly encouraging them to visit. Lack of means wasn't the issue the problem was neither of them had been out of the country and were both nervous of going on a plane but I could feel all my Dad needed was a push and if he came my mother would have to follow as there was no alternative for a couple who had not spent a night apart except when my mother was in hospital having us.

I wrote to my sister Nora first hoping she would gently break the news but she was having none of it.

15 Dartmouth Square
Dublin 2

Dear Kayleigh,

I might as well let you know Mum and Dad are not at all happy about this up and coming wedding. Is it really necessary for you to get married? It's such a huge step especially here in Ireland where there's no divorce. Sorry to be so optimistic but these things are worth considering under the usual circumstances but in your case because of the huge cultural differences and the short length of time that you know each other. Besides we don't even know what he looks like - how do you expect us to make up our minds about him without a photo after all in Ireland marriage is a family decision----I believe it's the same in rural China.

Dear Nora

I can see there was no point in trying to get you to gently pave the way for me. Always the one for a bit of drama but you'll be glad to know you'll meet your match in China. Obviously such things transcend culture. I enclose a photo of my dear Chi perhaps that will settle the matter finally.

Dear Kayleigh,

I chose to ignore your disparaging remarks about my innocent sisterly concern for your well being. But I must say the photo settles the issue for me and the rest of the clan --he's only gorgeous does he have any brothers, distant relatives, friends??????

PS I'd better warn you Dad is going to phone you.

After many frustrating attempts Dad manages to communicate to the college operator that he wants extension san, er, wu (three, two and five). Each time he got through he got brutally caught off by a crusty Chinese operator. Whether in the end she understood his Chinese intonation or she just figured he must be looking for the *wai gou ren* (foreigner) who knows but he got through anyway.

'You know we only want the best for you.'

'But I really love this man.'

'But marriage is such a huge step.'

'I know Dad but I am sure.'

'There was silence on the other end of the phone.'

My Dad had hung up on me!

I phoned back and eventually got through to Mum. She said he was just in a state of shock. He would come round. I was in a state of shock. I'd forgotten Dad's have feelings too. He was always there; a pillar to lean on, a bastion in times of storms, a comfort in times of pain, it was a shock to the system that I found it difficult to believe he couldn't support me now. In the end they decided they couldn't come. The journey and excitement would be too much for my dad's heart. I was secretly relieved. Who after all would want the responsibility of their father's heart on their shoulders. But they sent my sister Nora as an ambassador for the family and she was enough to handle with all the other preparations for the wedding.

What was the point of having a Chinese wedding Chi had debated if we did not have the traditional ritual type one. The modern banquet was so bland by comparison that many young couples were opting for it.

'My family in the countryside would be delighted to organise it' he said hugging me close to him.

Funny thing memory, it brings close what was far away and can maintain a distance from what is near. The retreat to the cock loft might have only occurred a few moments ago it feels that real to me and yet I know a huge wave of events have intervened. As the bride to be I retreat to the cock loft in accordance with Chinese traditional customs with my sister Nora, my best friend Molly, and Li Li, Chi's younger sister. The loft is an old Chinese style house in Guanxi village. The house belonged to Chi's eldest sister Guo Wei. According to tradition, Chi and the other members of his family were at his aunt's house. It is a small room with the low eves of the ceiling almost touching our heads. We are lying on the bed sipping cups of green tea Nora, Molly, Li Li and I.

'This was called the cock loft' says Li Li 'because this was where the chickens were kept in ancient times and this was where the bride usually stayed until the morning of her wedding.'

'Usually her best friends or sisters sang sad songs because she was leaving the family. They even cursed her parents for letting her go.'

'Well, I don't think Molly or I will be doing that, ' laughs Nora.

'Well first of all I don't even know any Chinese curses. Can you tell us some Lili?

'I don't think so,' says Li Li 'you might use it against me.'

'Ah come on,' Molly persisted, 'what are they like? Are they usually to do with sex like ours?'

'Yes but that's all I'm telling you.'

'Like F_ _ _ you?' spells Nora

But Gou Wei wasn't to be drawn out.

'Sorry, I don't know what you mean. I'll sing you a sad love song to lament Kayleigh.

Totally spontaneously, taking us all by surprise, Li Li sings a Chinese lament for the loss of the family's daughter as is the Chinese tradition. It resonates in the peculiar wailing of Chinese folksong whose lonesome melody finds no parallel except perhaps in the keening women's song of the old Irish wake. The floors vibrated and the thick walls drank in the weeping tune which cursed the mother and father for leaving their daughter go and her friends forlorn.

Thankfully it did not have the requisite fifty verses of the Irish wake song but ended quite abruptly with Li Li putting he hands to her face and dropping her head to her knees where we sat on the bed.

'That sounded very mournful,' says Nora, 'What was that all about?'

'It's the lament of the friends of the bride for the loss of their friend, says Li Li. It curses the mother and father for letting her go.'

'We don't have anything like that in our culture,' says Molly and we've been thought to believe that the Chinese culture doesn't value girls.'

'What's more here in China the groom's family are supposed to pay a dowry for the women whereas in Ireland it was the other way round.' I interject.

'Yeah, says Nora, 'in the Irish countryside the woman usually ended up being the unpaid servant inside and outside the house.'

'I do not agree with foot binding, says Li Li, but at least it saved the women from some of the harder work in the fields unlike our sisters in other Asian countries.

'You Chinese have such beautiful voices.' says Nora.

'But so have you Irish please Miss Molly will you sing for us?'

'How about it will not be long love 'til our wedding.' I suggest.

'Oh that's a bit lonesome' interjects Nora. 'How about something more appropriate to me like, How would it be if I died an old Maid in the garret?'

'What meaning does that have?' asks Li Li

'Oh, it's a funny song about a woman worrying about if she'll end up not married. Do you worry about that?'

'Oh, every Chinese worry about that.' Li Li responds

'Well you better sing it so Molly' shout Nora.

After the song the mood changed and Li Li sensing this got up off the bed saying, 'Lovely singing Molly but now time for bed. Miss Kayleigh have big day tomorrow she need rest.'

'I'm really nervous with all these rituals I'll do something wrong. I'm feeling very giddy.' I confide now that they are leaving.

'I know' says Nora, 'she's giddy at the best of times.'

'What means giddy? says Gou Wei looking confused.

'Nervous, always moving,' says Molly, 'and so we say as giddy as a goat.'

'Oh do not worry, you'll be fine.' says Li Li. 'Just do like the practice.' 'And tonight we have some herbal tablets to help you sleep. There take some of this with water. They are very relaxing but not too strong.'

And she hand me some chunky murky green tablets from a dark brown jar.

'Can I. have some too?' asks Molly

'Of course you can for this special occasion.'

Despite my outer pretence of joviality I was very nervous of my ability to perform like a demure Chinese girl on the day

I didn't feel either dainty or serene like the ideal prospective bride. In fact I felt clumsy and gitterbuggy. It was useless to talk about this to Molly she taught it was all just a laugh anyway and Nora was even more nervous than I which was a good thing really since she kept me preoccupied...

I decided to meditate to help me sleep and also to get Nora and Molly to stop cackling into the early hours of morning they giggled and huffed but the tablets must have worked because soon I had peace.`

It must have been one of my best meditations ever.

I did the meditation through the third eye and I could see a purple eye with a violet iris. My mind focused on the eye and soon the light started to revolve in a vortex of colour the movement and the light held me suspended in bliss tranquillity and calm and I felt a rush of love to my heart. I heard myself call out mother in Chinese and I flee secure happy and safe.

The lights continued to revolve in a spectrum from green to blue to yellow to purple it was serene it was beauty it was love. I felt very happy and deep in the realisation that true happiness is in lightness about life not taking myself so seriously and I vowed before I fell asleep not to take myself too seriously again - some hope.

I fell asleep with sweet dreams of Chi.

The morning of the wedding Lili washes my hair in citrus smelling water. First she massages my scalp in soothing circular motions, and then she gently pours the water over and squeezes it dry, patting it gently with a warm towel.

'We don't wash the hair just rinse it in a pumelo infusion' says Lili.

'So that's what it's called I thought it was some kind of grapefruit.'

'Well yes it's a type of grapefruit; it's supposed to cleanse bad influences.'

'Well I do feel fantastic after it'

'Here's another basin' says Guo Wei coming up from

downstairs with an enamel bowl steaming with the same fruity scent.

'And a wash cloth and a drying clothe for your body wash. We'll leave you alone to bathe and we'll be back up soon to do your costume and your hair.'

'Thank you thank you for everything I feel so relaxed after that head massage and hair infusion.'

I strip off my night clothes secure in the privacy of the windowless loft, a rare treat in densely populated China.

I am not as nervous as I anticipated but a wonderful feeling of elation transported my hormones onto a different plane of existence, perhaps it was the herbs from the night before, even the Mao Tai, the gentle head massage, the pumelo. But as I slowly watched the water flow over my body for the last time as a single woman I knew it was the security I felt that I was making the right choice, I had never before felt so close to any one person never felt so much love for one person, never wanted to be with anyone as much in my life and yet in a curious way I also knew I could live with separation from him, a separation that came as a premonition on my marriage day. Yet I knew we were strong enough to withstand such separation.

My greatest fear today is that the rituals will be too much for me that I will stumble, crumble my way through in my awkward gangly way. Not that I am really tall but the Chinese women are as petite and delicate as the etchings on their fans.

I have always been casual in my approach to life and formal rituals leave me cold but so far I am amazed at how relaxed I am with the Chinese rituals, perhaps it's because they are the rituals of another culture I feel myself outside and inside them at the same time. And of course the humorous way in which the Chinese approach things make them lighter.

I am startled out of my reverie by the sound of Lili's return to the chamber

I quickly dry myself and wrap the towel loosely around me.

'We think one person enough to help you dress- too many people too much fuss.'

Oh you are so thoughtful, that does give me the chance to compose myself for the day

I am inwardly delighted that neither Molly nor my sister are fluttering around me like dragonflies this morning there is enough chatter and nerve power between them to electrocute me.

I can even feel the energy surge from their room downstairs as they clattered and chattered about in their bare feet.

Lili must have sensed my unease as she put on a wonderful cassette of traditional Chinese song in the background and began to hum along as she dressed me in an expert caress, first in a soft cotton vest and then in a qi pao, a traditional symmetrical tunic of tradion buttoned to one side.

'The style suits you Lili remarks sincerely. It shows off your curves and small waist and the slits let everyone see your lovely legs.'

'Oh keep going keep going Lili.'

'Compliments are like dessert to me, though if wore this in Ireland my mother would insist I have the slit sewn up.'

'No cannot do that,' Lili laughed, 'and then you would not be able to move

Now what way do you want your hair? It is customary to have it up.'

'Yeah, it will be good to have it out of the way.'

'I'll let some hang from the sides and I have some decorations and flowers to put in too as I say some lucky words for you.'

Lili's incantations worked into my head like a trance. I felt like a queen being crowned and my third eye started to pulse slightly, forcing me to close my eyes with the sensation as shooting rays of golden light started to fill up my head. And I am transported to last night's dream of playing underwater volleyball with my new Chinese friends and family. Chi is to the fore tossing the ball playfully at me a big cheeky grin on his face then suddenly we all start to emerge from the water so that we are all waist deep in water and hitting the ball above water. Chi takes on the shape of my brother and the others my sisters and friends from home but my Irish family and friends are speaking Chinese. I begin to wonder at the significance of this dream and vow to tell Chi and then I remember where I am.

When I opened my eyes again the hair was complete and the headpiece of gold and silver felt indeed like a crown. Every woman should be queen for at least a day.

From that moment on I seemed to be walking on air, carried effortlessly by a light breeze of golden and silver light with the sweet hum of Chinese music in my ears. My sister's nervous chatter and Molly's buoyant boomerang personality only bounced off me and I was unaffected.

Lili pleaded to Guo Wei in mock Chinese tradition not to take me away from my loving family but Guo Wei gathered me up in her arms as was the custom and carried me downstairs on her back to the living area where Molly and Nora were waiting.

Gou Wei put a red silk veil around my face in keeping with tradition.

'Well that will keep her quiet for a while.' says Nora.

Qi's story

Mean while I am being dressed in a long gold gown, red shoes and a red silk sash with a silk balloon the shoulder by my brother Zhou. He is a good brother with a steady hand. He is also an initiate of Lao Yu and together we meditate in front of the family after and once more I receive a vision of Lao Yu and she is smiling at me. I know Kayleigh and I have the benefit of karma and the fates and destiny and it is our destiny to be together across the divide of culture and time. It is amazing that both parents have come to accept our union despite the differences of culture and country. My own father is so traditional I never thought he would agree to a foreign wife but then as my mother pointed out she herself was not Chinese but a minority Muslim.

I think personally it was meeting Kayleigh in person that persuaded him, a spring blossom bringing fresh hope.

I hope she is not too over whelmed by the rituals today. We tried to simplify things because I know she doesn't like formality but in a way it is easier to have some ritual at least you have a guide for behaviour.

Of course a lot of it is just for fun like this ridiculous cap I have to wear with cypress leaves coming out of the head.

Even my father is smiling.

'Son I never thought you'd agree to wear that hat' he said. 'It looks just as silly on you as it did on me those many years ago but it will give you a light head and a light heart.' I bow to him and to the alter of my ancestors saying, 'father thank you for all you have given and especially for your humour to this day'. With that my father removes the silk ball from my sash and my mother, two brothers, brother in-law and best friend Zhang and Duan follow him outside to the bridal sedan chair which is covered completely in red satin and white flowers. It is a glorious spring morning. The sunshine in Northern China in the spring is spectacular. Some of our group have decided to don the modern look, dark sunglasses and Zhua fits a pair on me. I am delighted for the comfort they afford and they seem to offer some protection from the den of firecrackers, loud gongs and drums that greet our ears outside. It booms out the last remaining consciousness of sleep and sends us into the public domain. It is after all a public day, a day of great celebration of young love. I am to lead the procession accompanied by my Brother Zhou's son Xin Xin to bring good luck to me in having sons in the future. Though that was a preoccupation of the past and does not bother me-children can wait-we must enjoy our love for each other.

We are followed by a colourful and raucous loud group of attendants carrying banners and lanterns, musicians of traditional music with flutes and lutes and a dancing lion.

At last we are at the bride's house the excitement is too much to bear but the sight of my two sister's, Molly and Nora all smiling relaxes me 'I see Molly and Nora have been well tutored by my sisters for the occasion.' The red pockets of money being offered symbolically for the bride by Zhou and Duan are scoffed at. Molly has even the audacity to throw the packets back in Zhou's face.

'Take that' she says in good Chinese, 'it is an insult to my friend.'

'Zhou and Duan are an equal match.'

'Oh so sorry little sister,' they say,' it was just a joke to test your sincerity.'

'Here we have a bag of gold for you' and they take out a heavy bag from the sedan chair which seems to be weighing them down.

'Not enough' says Nora 'I will need one of these too after all the sisterly love I have given over the years'

But Zhou and Duan retort;

'Oh sister don't be so hard on us. After all we have come far and the money is heavy to carry. But for you we have this special gold chain in memory of your sister's love'

As Duan puts the chain around Nora's neck we see many sparkles in her eyes.

'Enough' says Guo Wei or 'we'll have another wedding to pay for.' 'Now it is time to bring you your bride' and she escorts Kayleigh in.

Gou Wei my elder sister was chosen as KayLeigh's good luck woman because she had two sons. She's a strong lady so it isn't difficult for her to carry Kayleigh on her back to the sedan chair. I can't see KayLeigh's face but I can hear her giggling underneath her veil.

And Nora and Molly whisper, don't drop her now she's come this far already.'

Off go the firecrackers again to frighten away evil spirits and the commotion is deafening.

The curtains are drawn on the sedan chair and I lead the procession to my parent's house followed by Kayla in the sedan chair.

The firecrackers lambaste us at the door. My father and mother and the rest of my family are waiting to greet us and receive Kayleigh.

Kayleigh has to step over a saddle to cross the threshold. I lead her by the hand. Lili strains a heap of rice in a sieve over KayLeigh's head to strain out evil spirits and a lucky mirror is shone by Gou Wei on KayLeigh's veil and finally I can lift it and behold my bride.

'Heaven, heaven' is all I can manage to mutter.

Chapter 10: Honeymoon in Turfan.

After the flurry of the wedding Kayleigh and Chi were delighted to be escaping away out West. They had chosen Chi's homeland of Xingjian, which shared the Western frontier with Tibet for their honeymoon. Along with Tibet it was one of the remotest and least populated parts of China. To get there they had to take the train across treeless Gansu with its big bouldery brown mountains, terraced where possible for growing, by farmers trying to eke out a living from its uninhabitable land.

The train, in Chinese known as the iron rooster, was still run on steam.

'They have stopped making these steam engines,' he said, as he put his arm around her for the first time in public, while they sat looking out at the scenery from the train window.

'They used to make them in Dalian up until last year, who knows how long more we will see them in our China,' His eyes gazing deeply into hers.

'All the more romantic to be on one now with you,' she returned his gaze dreamily.

And he cuddled her more closely to him as he whispered in her ear, 'I love these old trains just as I love you. They have a real heart to them, a heart on fire like the heart of love.'

She snuggled up close to him as she whispered with a giggle,

'And I love their rhythm, echoing the rhythm of love, '

They both laughed in unison and soon the train spluttered to a slower pace.

'I'd better get up to get some *kai shui* to slow me down,' she said otherwise I'd be all over you soon'

'The same for me too' he said as he gave her a hand to get up.

Just then the train came to a grinding halt and flung Kayleigh into the arms of a nearby official.

The young official just laughed,

'Ha foreign friends not used to Chinese trains,'

and he returned her to Chi who had leaped to break her fall.

'But why are we stopping there is no station?' she turned to Chi.

'It is probably a junction with another train coming through.' He replied in that reassuring tone of voice that she loved that made her feel safe in the world.

Sure enough a freight train went trundling past.

'I think I'll sit down until we get going again and she smooched into the cradle of his arm.

'How far are we now from your friends town?' she had to look up at him to ask.

'I estimate another four hours' he whispered soothingly. 'What is the word again in English for cave dwellers?'

'Oh troglodytes..... to be honest I never knew the name until I saw it in the guide book such a prehistoric kind of word......' and her voice tapered off as if into a dream.

'I suppose it is a prehistoric type of home. The original home of our ancestors, the cavemen' and he growled into the hollow of her neck.

She erupted in giggles.

The couple were waiting for them at the tiny station, lingering in a harmonious stance. They were newly weds too, Liu and Ming. Both middle school teachers, assigned to the countryside. Chi had met them in college in Beijing. They seemed very much in love and very cheerful.

As they walked to their home they fell in line together for a chat

'At first we didn't like the idea of being sent to the countryside,' says Ming, 'but at least we are posted together.'

They are so gentle and serene, Kayleigh mused, was it living so close to the earth, she wondered.

The house was surprisingly cosy inside but noticeable cool

along the walls. There was coal stove lighting in the centre and a chimney outlet. The walls were painted green and the floor was concrete. Kayleigh was delighted to help Ming with the evening meal of jaoize, steamed pork and vegetable dumplings. It was one of the meals she had had practice cooking with her students so she felt quite adept. She loved the communality of the cooking, rolling out the pastry while Ming chopped up the filling and of course it gave them ample time to chat while the boys went off shopping in the local market for food for breakfast.

'Do the Western men help much around the house? Asked Ming

It depends on the man and whether the woman is working outside the home or not. In my country, Ireland I'd say the women do most of the housework but times are changing.

Chinese men generally like cooking though in the farms women still do a lot of it. If the two people are working outside the farm as in our case, the men help out a lot. And with the children too.

Oh here they come. Ming was just saying how wonderful Chinese men are in the home.

That's so true says Chi.

You two lovely ladies sit down while I pour the beer and Liu will serve the dinner. Just relax and enjoy.

Kayleigh and Ming passed a very relaxing evening waited on hand and foot whilst talking about the conditions for women in China.

She learnt things had really improved for women under communism with the abolition of foot binding and concubines. Women were allowed to be educated and use modern birth control. She was delighted that both Chi and Liu agreed that women should have equal rights as men. She stored all this in her memory and that night in a little room off the main living room she slept secure in his love.

After a morning breakfast of xiao mian bao, (steamed white bread) and green tea they said their goodbyes at the train station to the sound of the belching, spluttering train.

'The Chinese train truly deserves its name,' laughs Liu, 'hot and steamy like a fire engine.' Ming pushed melons and other edibles into Chi's arms and they waved goodbye with loneliness languishing in the air.

The train huffed and puffed its way along the route of the old Silk Road that once stretched from Arabia into China bringing trade and commerce east west. It travelled in fits and starts speeding up and slowing down to a rickety momentum. The *Huo che*, fire vehicle, took them through miles and miles of mud walled towns, along a green valley enclosed by large brown mountains. In the distance was an even higher range of snowy peaks. Chi said they were about 20,000 feet high. Kayleigh was awe struck at the magnitude and range of the land.

'We have entered Xingjian province,' said Chi. 'Now you can see why it is not populated.'

'Is it all desert then?' She asked amazed.

'There are oases along the way; you will see the train stopping at them. The route is known as the arm of the Silk Road. The people in the oases make their living from trade with the passing tribes. The Kazaks are still nomadic and make their living from herding sheep in the grasslands in the mountains. The Uigurs, my mother's people are mainly settled farmers. So you see why it is so thinly populated even though it is one sixth of China's land area, desert and mountain mainly, that is our Xingjian..

Soon they were swept into silence by the expanse of it: staring into its hypnotic sway from the carriage window. Across the desert through the desert sky they see the vast nothingness of the sea in the vastness of sand. Grains of sand like tiny grains of human folly stretching out as far as the eye can see.

The desert will always be a mystic place, Kayleigh thought, a place of resolution, evolution. Was there not always desert? She wondered, the desert itself seems like eternity. Hard to believe that this was one day under the sea and yet the desert land is a seascape, its undulating waves a mystery as vast and deep as any ocean.

It mesmerised her into a mystical trance. It reverberated with questions of a soul-seeking kind. Together with Chi she searched its sands for the grains of truth left over from its storms. And in the tranquillity and succour of its oasis at Turfan, Chi's birthplace, they learnt that the song of the surrounding desert was the lover's song, carried in the gentle sweep of the desert winds across the silence of the sands.

Turfan was the home of Chi's mother's people, the Uigurs. His father had been sent there as an agricultural advisor and became enamoured with the people and their ways. It was to the home of his Muslim ancestors Chi decided to return for their honeymoon since this was where he felt most at home. It is the lowest place below sea level in China, 155 metres deep. Established over two thousand years ago as an important Oasis on the road it had gone into decline with the decline of the route itself.

They arrived in the early evening, shaken, dusty and bone weary from the rambunctious ride. Kayleigh could feel the desert sand in her eyes and in her hair, under her fingernails and even on her mouth. They smiled and heaved in unison, relief at the journey's end. The station was at the edge of the depression. Breathing down on them were the Flaming Mountains, aptly named for their red glow. Along route to the town which was only twenty lei away the broad expanse of bouldery and brown desert was interrupted by telegraph poles. Every now and then big mounds of sand were piled high.

To Kayleigh they looked like huge ant hills and Chi laughed when she asked if that was what they were.

'Ay yah,' he exclaimed, no, no. They are part of the irrigation system. They are holes dug to give access to the irrigation canals to repair them. The canals stretch from the mountains to the oasis. The snow melts in the mountains and the water is brought to Turfan along the canals since ancient times, over two thousand years ago.' The vines are threatened by sub zero cold in winter and wind driven sands that for three months in spring. The winds called black hurricanes bury people in their homes for days.

After the long rickety, dusty ride Kayleigh was enchanted. A beat up old taxi took them from the train station to the nearby town. Snake charming music wafted from its crackling radio. The cab driver was a big swarthy Arab-looking man and he seemed completely nonplussed when Chi told him they were on honeymoon in native dialect. She sees his eyes investigate her through his sunglasses in the driver's mirror.

Chi joked, 'He says you are pretty but too thin - you need to eat more.'

They laughed. 'Doesn't worry tell him I've a huge appetite from all that travelling? And I can't wait to try the local food.'

The town itself was a real delight. Approaching it Kayleigh thought it looked like an enormous green cavern. In fact the streets were enveloped in a series of trellises overhung by grape vines.

'It does look like a mirage, a paradise lost in the desert' she exclaimed.

'And you will look like a mirage to the people here, since they rarely see foreigners' Chi says.

As they entered the arbour Kayleigh felt immediate relief from the overwhelming heat in the cab, despite all the windows being down.

The streets were lined with houses made of abode; straw and mud mixed in Arabic style. As they alighted from the cab Chi grabbed a bunch of grapes and held them dangling above her mouth. She hesitated.

'Go on, eat.' he said. 'They belong to the house.'

To Kayleigh they tasted succulently sweet, the fruit of paradise, bringing a swift recovery from the journey.

They were to stay with Chi's aunt and uncle and their family. At the arched white doorway they were waiting with swarthy Muslim welcomes. They spoke Uigur to Chi whilst all the while giving Kayleigh warm smiles. They were shown to their rooms to rest before supper that night. The cold shower of sweet scented grape water ran the dust from every molecule of skin, every cornice and curve of their bodies. And they bathed together in the assurance that the waters flow hid their laughter and their bodily play.

That evening Chi's uncle and aunt had prepared a veritable feast for the newly weds. They slaughtered a lamb for the occasion and their two sons swung it from a giant skewer and brought it out to the awaiting guests in the courtyard for display before retiring to the kitchen to chop it up. Two female cousins came from the kitchen singing a Uigur honeymoon song. Dressed in traditional costume one carrying the Hada, the Muslim scarf of welcome and the other a tray of silver white wine glasses. They danced and sang their way around the guests offerings the potent drinks and wrapping the scarves around the two guests of honour who stood up to receive them. Soon after they returned with the food steaming on platters for the hotpots of flavoured coriander soup kept simmering in the centre of the tables by little gas stoves underneath. Lamb and green vegetable and sauces were laid at each guest's side to be cooked in the bubbling stew to the appetites desire. Freshly baked white yeast bread was added for the filling. The balmy summer air, the wafts of sweet lamb, the strong local wine, and the garrulous company sent Kayleigh's head into a heady spin from which their was no returning and she could see from his eyes that it had the same effect on Chi and indeed on the rest of the family. The feasting continued long into the summer's night with more songs and music to follow. Kayleigh was even encouraged into a rendition of an old Gaelic song *Oro 'se do Beatha Bhaile* for which she was heartily applauded whilst Chi sang an ancient Uigur love song that stole her heart yet again. They retired into the night still singing in their beds.

The next morning as she lay next to Chi, skin to skin, the singing swimming in her head, the somnambulant heat lending a sensual air Kayleigh mused that nothing about the place felt like China. To her it felt pure Arabic. It was so hot that the sweat evaporated from their skin as soon as it was expressed, even in bed under the cool of the fan. Without Chi's continual vigilance about drinking water Kayleigh would have often come dangerously close to dehydration. The next day in the market place she came close to a swoon on a number of occasions except she had Chi's hand to grasp as he gently put the water canister to her lips. She had been so mesmerised by the oriental exoticness of the bazaar that she'd forgotten about the heat. According to Chi it had once been one of the largest on the silk route but it went into decline around the sixteenth century.

'Different nomadic tribes had control over Turfan at different times, since it was established over two thousand years ago. Tibetans, Mongols, Kazaks. Today it's my mother's people the Uigurs.' he expanded.

These peoples were all in evidence that day bartering and trading as of old. Most of the people looked Middle Eastern, not Chinese. They were dark skinned, had large round eyes and the prominent noses of the Arabic look. Some of the men wore the Muslim skull cap, others wore the elaborate headdress more prominent among the Tibetans. The women were even more colourful still, .They wore vibrant bold silks of red and yellow, and elaborate gold and silver jewellery; bangles, chains and earrings. They had large bosoms and were just as forward as the men in demanding a sale and offering a bargain As they walked through the winding dusty route of the stalls the place took upon more and more the appearance of a central Asian bazaar. Embroidered saddlebags, leather holsters, home made jack knives, baskets, belts and jewellery hanging from tented stalls in one section and food selling in another; mutton and lamb, dried fruit raisins, apricots, almonds and walnuts. Here and there fire eaters, contortionists and card wizards found space to amuse the crowds.

Chi bought a beautiful; silver torc with an aqaumarine

stone and fastened it around Kayleigh's neck. How did you know it's my favourite stone? she asked.

'It just seems to suit you so well. It's also supposed to be a great stone for healing.'

'Thank you it will always make me think of you.'

She found him a lovely gold and amber ring.

'I was always fascinated by amber,' he said, 'it tells the story of millennia from the sap of the tree of life and the life embedded in it. This ring will unite our lives forever.'

Another day they went by taxi to visit the ruins of the ancient city of Gaocheng, twenty five miles east of Turfan. Little remained of the ruined city except piles of dust and crumbling walls. What remained revealed it had been a city on a grand scale, a citadel, though most of its walls and fortifications were now gone with only the sun beating down on the mud bricks and dusty walls. Some of the buildings were just irregular mounds of sandy mud whilst others had a more definite structure. It was as if the desert had recouped the city for itself drawing it back to its smothering sands. Kayleigh felt light headed in the heat and dizzy with the sight of the remains of the desert. It gave herself and Chi a shuddering sense of their own mortality and the transience of their earthly love.

They rested in the shade of the city's stumbling walls, guzzling water from their canister, and gazed at the dilapidation of what was once a glorious city. A hot desert wind stirred her out of her stupor and Kayleigh turned to Chi and said,

'It is one thing to see an abandoned house and ....to sense the loss of the generations of one family..... that may have lived there...... But it is another experience entirely to experience a deserted city where whole generations of people have been wiped out.'

'Yes.' said Chi, 'and the different tribes who have lived in this city, Han Chinese, Tibetan, Mongols, Uigurs and Kazaks, all gone. It's almost as if the wind is blowing their ghosts through these walls.'

'Stop Chi, now you are really making me shudder even in the heat.'

'I think its time to take that taxi back,' says Chi shaking them out of their reverie.

'We'll be fried meat by the time anyone gets here,' she said.

'Don't worry we have lots of relatives who would miss us.'

'Even so don't want to be here with Mongolian ghosts after dark.'

Yet they remained leaning in the shade of a tumbling mud wall dazing out at the vastness of the sands their minds melted together into a universal poetry of the desert;

ethereal
ephemeral
creatures of light and dust
temporarily
passengers of time
grasping with substantial hands
at forever
shooting stars on a race
against time
and gravity
personality and conflict
fingerprinting
in black holes
interspersed through the millennia by light

Suddenly their taxi appeared in a cloud of dust and sputtering engine sound and startled them out of their united unconscious.

'Better get back before the dark,' he shouted in Uigur, 'don't want to end up like this town eh?'

On the journey back as sun set quickly over the horizon they knew they would never forget these lovely languid early days in the desert when the heat stretched out the hours into the elongated shadows of the evening, that deep sensual heat of mirages that made reality an illusion and anything sensual possible, the heat in the depth of night with fiery stars over head and the restless sleep as their bodies rippled around the sand dunes of love and time. It was a place to which they would always return whether in dream or reality together.

Chapter Eleven: The Way of Lao Yu, the Avatar.
We know by going where we are going to.

The mountain was steep and the path that Chi was showing me was worn and dusty. The countryside was a sea of green and lined with trees of varieties I had never seen before. It was the autumn of the year and I remarked that most of them seemed deciduous except along the tops of the hills where more lustrous evergreens launched themselves.

Leaves of gold, red, and yellow drifted across our pathway lapped up by a playful wind.

At the top of the pathway we were met by Lao Yu and a group of her followers. They were dressed in the traditional Taoist robes, long tunics composed of a patchwork of brocaded silk quilted together in harmonising hues of blue, complimented by navy skull hats that fitted neatly on their heads and velvet shoes of blue over loose fitting navy trousers.

They greet us with the customary 'Wai', hands joined together in prayer and the head gently bowed in respect. We return the salute.

Lao Yu speaks first.

'You are very welcome to our holy mountain.
Chi has been coming here for sometime
and any friend of Chi's is welcome here.
We hope you will like our ways and
what we have to teach you
which of course you already know.'

I bow in thanks.

With a radiant face and subtle smile she continues:

'The mountains were always considered holy in ancient China

and so we have many famous Chinese holy mountains
which are home to Taoist and Buddhist monasteries.
Hua Lin Shan is one.
The mountains are closer to heaven
and provide the best environment to learn Qi Gong
the Chinese breathing that leads to good health and
harmony.'

As Lao Yu brings me through the basic Qi Gong steps I
find a quiet stillness well up inside me. The concentration
required throws all other thoughts out the window of my
mind.
You bring the energy up through your feet
inhale it like a breath up along the legs
through the torso
into the arms
as it shallows out.
Then breathe back down
from the head to the toes
in a circular motion
continuously focusing on the breath.

Now they are taking us to the Taoist Women's Temple.
Lao Yu says I can practice here as often as I wish. It is only
a one hour bicycle ride from Lanyuan.
The Temple is a monument to beauty in architecture. It is
painted red vermilion and is enclosed by red painted walls.
The arched entrance is sealed by heavy teak doors. Guarded
by statues of warrior deities who chase away approaching
evil.
The doors open into a courtyard where a spirit wall affords
further protection by blocking direct entry. The Chinese
believe that spirits cannot turn corners and thus the name is
derived.
Inside there is a succession of halls arranged in ornamental
courtyards the innermost being the main temple. Here we are

seated on silk brocade cushions rested on wooden floors facing Guanyin.

Although she is a Buddhist Goddess of Mercy statues of Guanyin are often found in Taoist halls as she is prayed to for assistance in child birth. She is multi-armed to cope with the multitude of petitions and carries a vase to distribute her healing waters.

Behind us on a rear wall are three statues of the Three Immortals of indecipherable sex each riding a crane a tiger and a deer. This Holy Trinity represents the three levels of the Taoist life

Hanging from the ceiling is an octagonal cupola sporting the black and white ying and yang symbol and between the black supporting pillars hang red drapes and red lanterns lending a radiant slow to the interior vestibule.

Lao Yu seats herself on a cushion under the cupola.

'Welcome comrades old and new.

I will give a brief talk so as not to bore the old or distract the new. She pauses to broaden her smile.

'According to Taoist teaching
the wise person or the sage
does not seek to conquer the world
but seeks to conquer oneself.
Does our new foreign friend understand my Chinese.
Chi will translate if you have a problem.'

'I am finding you surprisingly easy to understand.' I reply.

'And so it should be with what is already known.'
She smiles the smile of centuries of serenity and her speech glides along effortlessly.

'And so..... how does one conquer oneself ?' She eyes Chi for the answer.

By practising Taoist purification techniques of meditation and Qi gong one realises the Tao, one's place in nature, one's role in the great cosmology.

'And what then is the Tao?'

An older nun responds:

'The Tao that can be named is not the eternal name but in essence the way is the way of nature or the cosmos. Human thought and action that is in accordance with nature follows the way.'

'What is nature's constitution ?' and Lao Yu nods to the young nun by my side. The response is immediate.

'Nature consists of the polarity of ying and yang
the cosmic forces that are represented in nature as male and female
day and night
heaven and earth
sun and moon
body and mind
reason and intuition
conscious and unconscious.'

'And which of the principals is the dominant one?'

'Perhaps the yang principal.' replied Chi jokingly

'As you well know Chi both of the principals are equal and necessary.

When working in harmony they complement each other
just as the male complements the female.

Both are made to love and support each other.

Both poles are good when they harmonise with each other
but both show their evil side when harmony is lost.

The sage knows that the real source of ones strength lies within

In ones harmony with the cosmic forces of ying and yang.

Thus the wise one does not depend too much on worldly success for his self esteem since the ego may often be deflected through external obstacles over which one has no control.

Thus the sage knows that all of life is in a state of flux, of continuous change and does not seek to rely on a false stability.

The wise one accepts and adapts to the changes just as one accepts and accords with the seasons the sunshine that follows rain the snow that traps the flowing water.

So too the sage knows that only the relative things can be expressed in words and all descriptions are only comparisons.

All conceptual knowledge is relative and true knowledge comes from our intuition that which cannot be expressed - the great ineffable.'

Her words resonated with a truth that found its way in the blood that coursed through my veins and centred itself in my heart.

Lao Yu drew her cloaked blue arms together and joined her hands in the prayer position.

'Which brings us to the end of our words and concepts of wisdom today
and draws us towards the wisdom within
the wisdom to be found in the stillness,
the emptiness
and the quiet of meditation.
Let us all inhale deeply now
until the exterior body begins to quieten down
and journeys inward to the stillness within.'

I had travelled so far to find my home.

Here in the seclusion of a Taoist monastery on a Chinese holy mountain I felt finally at home on this earth.

I had found love
truth
wisdom
and peace.
I had found myself.

Some months later;

Only the red tiled roofs were visible in the early morning mists that draped the courtyard in a powder puff glow. As the cheeky rays of morning dissolved the mists, the silhouetted figures emerged slowly, lithely dancing as if suspended in the light. The bamboos that fringed the courtyard were beside themselves with delight at lending sanctuary to these nimble dancers as they displayed the versatility of their art; lightly leaping, slowly kicking, their arms following, as they circled the courtyard.

Lao Yu stood in the shade of the large bamboo that bent its leaves softly towards her. She looked out at the *outside country* (foreign) initiate that Chi had brought. She had been coming here now for several months, early in the morning for Tai Chi and Qi Gong and in the evening for meditation and lectures.

Was this her, finally? She wondered.

Was this the one who been chosen to spread The Way to the West?

Of course she would not be the only one. It was too mammoth a task for any one person but could she at least be one of them?

She could see Kayleigh's aura very clearly from where she waited with the patience of immortality. The predominant colour was the turquoise of communication, shimmering a distance of two feet in an oval shape around her body.

It was an incredibly good sign and the time was right, the period of the harvest.

The moon was at its zenith.

How appropriate that Chi would bring her here; he whose destiny would take him on a journey to the West. Lao Yu mused.

The coincidences were there to be read, the omens were good but one had always to thread the Way with caution and never be compelled by one's own eagerness for results. The

Rita Hogan

Way that is forced is not the real way.
And the Way that is in tune with the forces of nature may
often dictate the principle of non-action. (Wu Wei.)
Now it is time to observe with patience and assist her and
him in learning the skills needed to follow the Tao.
Yes, she is making good progress with the Tai Chi and Qi
gong exercises.

With focused attention Kayleigh follows the slow movements of the instructor and synchronises with the others in the class. Chi is part of the group. Sometimes she finds this distracting. There are times, however, like today when she can feel that union that the instructors talk about.

The union of the opposites that is the Tao.

She feels like she and Chi are part of the same body,
synchronised in the dance of life,
moving in a rhythm that connects them
to the other initiates in the monastery,
and reverberates out beyond the monastic walls
to the whole of the world,
the universe of life.

At times like this she feels like the boundaries between her body and the outer world do not exist.

She becomes one with the interchange of molecules between her body and the air around it;

the oxygen and water vapour exchanging for carbon dioxide in the lungs,

her skin cells intermingling with the moisture molecules of air,

and the laughing molecules of light.

It has taken her four months to achieve the meditational aspect of her Tai Chi training. First she had to master the movements, many of which are based on those of forest animals; like the monkey, the tiger and the snake. Legend has it that Tai Chi was taught to the Emperor Xuan Wu by an alchemist hermit in a dream. It is only when one has achieved a dream - like state, when the movements become unselfconscious, that the meditation spawns.

In the beginning even the starting stance felt very awkward for Kayleigh - it being so different from the normal standing pose.

The feet are shoulder width apart
and the knees are slightly bent.
A straight back is achieved - not by having the chest out
and the shoulders back -
but by rounding off the shoulders and the chest
and loosening the upper body completely.
So relaxed that the body feels like it's suspended in water.
All stress evaporates.

Moving on from the basic stance, the body's weight is shifted delicately
from one leg
to the other.
Simultaneously the arms are directed into graceful, ballet-like positions
with evocative names like
playing the lute
and
waving hands like clouds.

In line with the bodily movements,
the breath is consciously directed
downwards
towards the dian tian,
(the solar plexus)
a point about ten inches above the navel.
Then up and out in a deep exhale.

The concentration is so focused that the only consciousness is the consciousness of the body breath in the dian tian, following this strange sequence of movements foreign to it's usual direction.

With practice the movements become more natural until one feels like Kayleigh today.

Yes it's just me in the movement of repulsing the monkey.
I am my body.
I am the movement.
But in the moment of recognising it I loose it.
This is it. Thinks Kayleigh.
This is where it's at.
Really being in my body.
Conscious only of the movements of the body
and that of the instructor
and the other students.

Here in the centre of the group I feel all the power of the group.
A surge of energy but not an energy I can't handle.
Energy through me and around me like a soft stream.
Soothing.
Refreshing.
Flowing.

The Qi Gong exercises follow the Tai Chi. Although primarily breathing exercises they are supported by massage and visualisation techniques. The Taoists believe that the control of the breath is essential for proper body functioning. The *qi* or breath is the body's vital energy which can be regulated at will by the art of Qi Gong. Lao Yu talks the group through one of the primary visualisation exercises.

Standing in the starting stance
Exhale to emit all the stale air
Breathe in and as you breathe in
Imagine your breath is coming up from the earth
Into your feet
Going up along your legs
Up the trunk of your body

Out along the arms
Into the neck
Up the head.
Exhale and as you exhale
Imagine the breath
Going down from the head
Into the neck
Along the arms
Down into the trunk of the body
Down into the legs
And back into the earth.
Repeat.

With each inhale Kayleigh could feel her body flooding with life, filling up simultaneously with gilded yellow light.
It was exhilarating but a bit unnerving.
Can I handle this new reality? Where is it taking me? Will I feel separate from friends and family now?
Still she luxuriated in the glow of energy.
She felt lightened and enlightened.

'The meditation makes one receptive to the philosophy. Only when the mind has achieved the level of receptivity nurtured by meditation can the philosophy of the Tao take hold. Today I am going to teach you a secret but this secret is no secret because you already know it. So are you willing to learn this secret you already know, the knowledge of good health and sound mind?'

Lao Yu's audience responded in captive union; 'We are.'

'Good health comes when you learn to forget yourself. When you think all the time about your problem it becomes more a problem. When you learn to forget your problem your problem will go away. This is the secret of meditation the ability to forget, to empty the mind, to become nothing. To feel nothing but the emptiness of the mind and finally the moment of stillness, nothingness, oneness with all. Of being a part of the whole that is the Tao.

The Tao must be experienced to be understood, be felt in order to be true. Meditation in its various forms, Tai Chi, Qi Gong, visualisation or through sound is the most effective way of achieving awareness of the Tao'

Lao Yu was speaking in the courtyard of the Western Goddess of the Earth

Kayleigh was there with the rest of the initiates dressed in a blue tunic. She shifted uncomfortably on her legs as she sat on the ground, still unused to the cross-legged sitting of the Chinese. The setting sun burst through the bamboo branches overhanging the courtyard spraying her head in a halo of its rays. Her hair lit up golden and Chi had to propel his eyes away from her. He prayed for their success.

Lao Yu continued.

'The Tao is not a creator God. It is not a God at all but the essence behind everything, the guiding principle, the source of all things. Yet it is not one thing. It is before the union of the opposites. It precedes it in time, but it gives rise to the union of opposites of ying and yang.'

She was perched serenely on a red brocade pillow looking calm and knowingly at Kayleigh and Chi. A slight smile betrayed a solemn occasion.

'Do you understand the relationship between Yin and Yang Kayleigh? Chi could you explain?'

As Chi turned towards her Kayleigh could see the brightness of wisdom in his eyes.

'The one created the two;
the opposites of yin and yang
which are constantly interacting in relationship with each other.

These polar opposites are represented in Nature as the male
and female
 though both the male and female have yin and yang
aspects.
 The predominance of one or the other leading to a
manifestation of one
 as opposed to the other.'

The small group sat on the flat earth coloured ground in a
circle. All blue robed in the prayer posture. Lao Yu chanted
the opening incantation. The group respond, their red beads
keeping the count. On the final invocation from behind Lao
Yu as if on cue a retinue in red robes is led by a bearer of a
voluminous tome. The young noviciate with the face of a
cherub places it delicately on its stand. The other young
monks give yarrow stalks to those seated in anticipation.
 'Exceptional times allow us to throw the I Ching in public.
These are such times. Chi and Kayleigh will ask the ancient
book of wisdom of their fate in following the Tao. We will
use the traditional method of throwing the yarrow stalks as it
is more refined and ceremonious than the modern method of
throwing coins'
 Lao Yu pointed with her blackbird eyes to Kayleigh and
Chi Hai O to come forward.
 'Since their fates are already bound together in love they
can throw the yarrow stalks together in one sitting. You will
throw in sequence, Kayleigh first. Prepare to meditate on your
query both of you.'
 Kayleigh and Chi looked first to each other and then to Lao
Yu as they breathed into their meditation in the centre of the
circle. Kayleigh was glad of the perceptible shading over of
the evening sun by the clouds. She felt herself blush with fear
and aliveness and her head was dizzy from the force of light
energy shooting in and out as she meditated on the question,
 Where will the Tao lead us?

She had never had this sensation before. It was like space age laser light shooting into her head from all angles lifting it and clearing it so that the question became the sole issue of focus. Chi was glad for the look of recognition that Kayla gave as he resided in his meditation. His head was full of purple light and he knew he was in the right place for asking questions so profound. Still he was also nervous because he knew there were the inevitable trials ahead as was the way of the world.

Eventually after many throws the fifty stalks composed themselves into Hexagram 51 of the I Ching.

Lao Yu divined its meaning

'The wisdom of the ancient oracle speaks of *Times of Turmoil* ahead. It advises that a person's attitude can make the difference between success and failure in these circumstances. Although it is necessary to take precautions and to look ahead with some concern there is no need to panic or to fret. In the same upheaval one may lose some privileges or possessions but may also encounter unexpected opportunities and in the end may gain. For manoeuvring in chaotic circumstances we need an alert and flexible attitude. If we lose our mental clarity or cling to preconceived ideas each new change will add to our confusion and get us deeper into the mire. But a calm and adaptable mind can easily handle the shocks that would cause most people to panic.

Indeed,' said Lao Yu, 'this is not the first time in recent years that the Oracle has foretold a time of great upheaval but ultimately the reading is positive in your favour.'

With that she rang the bell. The retinue returned for their treasure and the group wove silently out of the hall.

In the stillness of her room that night Kayleigh wondered about the reading and its consequences. She knew that her own worst enemy was indeed herself.

Oh, she mused, *the wise one knows that to conquer oneself is a far greeter deed than to conquer the world but that was a lot easier said than done.* She was worried about what she had gotten herself into now that she was so far involved in her training. She couldn't believe that the path to enlightenment could lead to such trails. In a way it was as tough as Catholicism cause you still had to face the terrible times with fortitude and calm; be strong, something she felt she had never been. The only thing with Taoism was at least you acquired the skills for bravery and cool collected thinking through the meditation, breathing and Tai Chi.

More difficult again than the spiritual aspect was the Tao of love. What advice really did the Tao give in this respect?

Balance and harmony.

But love by its very nature seemed unbalanced, fired as it was by the emotions which are difficult to harmonise. Her thoughts weighed her down
    down
    down
    into a heavy sleep
    and soared her into
    a light
    lightdream of Chi.
    The two of them were dressed in brilliant white
    back-lit by the brightness of the sun
    they were floating high over fields of golden corn
    dancing in a flight of golden love.
    Angels of light heralded
    by bells of joy.

Chapter Twelve:_The Poster Campaign

PROLOGUE

The largest and longest demonstration of popular democratic discontent in history was to be displayed not in the so-called Western democracies but in a country that was regarded in the West as a totalitarian dictatorship. Unknown to the Western public and indeed the world at large by May 1989 the demonstrations were general over every major Chinese city. Each had become a bastion of revolt, fortressed from within and without by a student population that had gained control of the cities' centres with the compliance of the authorities and the collaboration of the workers, the unemployed, the business people and the intellectuals.

By mid May day to day life was at a standstill; the protests had taken over the souls of the cities and they pulsed with a new fervour; a fervour of discontent with the way the country was being run was fuelled by a burning desire to govern the country in the best, the fairest way possible; a true humanitarian yearning to bring about an equal society with justice for all. A yearning ignited in the students souls by the very propaganda that was designed to subjugate them and make them subservient.

These were still the early days for Kayleigh; the naive sentimental days, when as yet she couldn't understand the cultural symbols of this extraordinary country and its people.

Looking back at it now it all had the bizarre inevitability of history. One event followed the other inexorably leading to the cataclysm; like the seemingly isolated but in retrospect connected incidents of a couple's history that led to the decline of their marrriage. But why the couple ask would such a sequence of incidents lead to the dissolution of our union while our friends, who have had far worse between them, are still together? So too the Chinese Government and indeed the people were asking in the wake of the terrible events of June 4 1989 why did it have to come to this disaster? Previous demonstrations by students in France, the US and in China had not had such mammoth results or consequences - what had precipitated this crisis? Remembering now her first steps in the country, the early conversations, the incidental incidents she can see how it all happened whilst never guessing that it would. And perhaps it was for her own best protection that she couldn't recognise all those cultural signs, but even if she could have would she have been just as startled as the Chinese Government by the tidal wave of events?

KAYLEIGH'S ACCOUNT

The first intimation that Julie and I had that there was something awry was when Dean Wu summoned us via Ming and Wei to his office on Monday morning before class. Ming and Wei could offer no clues as to what was up and this made us even more suspicious. Usually they had a nose to the ground feel of events, either they genuinely knew nothing or they had been ordered to play dumb. Anyway it was a strange turn of events as we had report meetings with Mr Wu on the last Friday of the month so what was the urgency behind this unscheduled summons?

There was no option but to wait until Monday morning. The tension in the office was as perceptible as chalk screeching on a well worn blackboard. It was obvious Ming and Wei were squirming behind their inscrutable face masks through which we could now see through as clearly as a crystal pool. We concluded that we were in for a reprimand because our students, who were inferior in rank (in a classless society) had been chosen to interpret rather than any one of our colleagues. That they had to translate in the first place was a sorry indictment of Mr Wu's teaching skills though he happily choose to believe it reflected more on our inability to grasp the language. All those tedious hours had obviously been time well spent by all parties. Those Chinese characters which he merrily attached to each object in the room had patently left no imprint whatsoever and Wu was too impatient to wait for us to regurgitate them anyway.

Despite his classes we had acquired a manageable grasp of Chinese but ironically he was the one Chinese person who protested he could not understand whatever his reasons. Most likely he schemed that we would continue paying him the outrageous fees for lessons. At this stage we would have paid not to have his classes or the irritation of his company but neither were luxuries that we knew how to contrive.

No attention was paid to the usual pleasantries of greetings like 'have you eaten?' or 'would you like some tea? It was clear Mr. Wu was taking himself very seriously indeed and he expanded his copious girth into his armchair to command the space in the room and it's occupants. His tone was solemn and he breathed heavily into each syllable. Intermittently he cleared his throat for added effect. I could absorb these details because I didn't need to concentrate on interpreting the strong Beijing accent which he prided himself on.

'The first point,' says Ming meekly, failing to convey the Dean's authoritativeness, 'is that Mr Wu say you show a video in class last Friday while he was away. Mr. Wu say video is not necessary for English class. He say this is only the way for the teacher to avoid her duty and it makes the class lazy. The students do not want videos because it introduce to them to decadent Western culture which is harmful to Chinese students.' She avoids looking at us but when she does she flashes an exaggerated innocence.

Impetuously as ever I begin to respond; 'but in out teacher training, video was considered an invaluable tool in language learning.'

Mr. Wu puts up his hand to stop me, angrily crashes his fist to the table and I understand his Chinese perfectly when he says he will not be interrupted.

His stampedes forward with his orders barely pausing for Ming's translation;

'In the future you will show no more videos. Instead you will give lectures on important figures in Western history, like Napoleon, Hitler and Winston Churchill.

You will also give lectures on science and technical subjects but not on religion or politics. Mr Wu asks if this clear?'

But before we have time to answer he steams ahead and Ming translates;

'You will give students essays to write on these topics and

you will correct them in you free time. Mr Wu say he expect you to obey him on this and he has no more to discuss. Please go to your classrooms now the bell is ringing.'

I don't know if my jaw has actually collapsed but that's the way if feels- myself and Julie look at each other and again at Mr. Wu incredulously and raise like automatons from our chairs. He dismisses us with a cold imperious stare.

'What the heck is going on?' I whisper in the corridor.

'I don't know' she says, 'but there's more to this than meets the eye.'

'I'm seeing Chi this afternoon after class. Do you want to come along he's bound to have some idea,' I suggest.

'Yes, thank you for inviting me, all this is making me extremely nervous.'

In a dimly lit small tea-house in the Muslim Quarter we asked Chi for his opinion of Mr Wu's behaviour. He listened intently as he usually did and after a considered pause for reflection over his steamy bowl of spiced tea he said.

'Yesterday Hu Yao Bong passed away. As you know he was one of our great leaders and loved by many people, especially the academics and students. He had a noble character; sincere, *honesty, integrity.* There has been an outpouring of grief by the public and spontaneous demonstrations in Beijing to honour him and to protest the Government's refusal to adopt his policies.'

'You mean this is influencing Mr Wu's behaviour here in Yuanlan, already?' Julie raises herself from her seat with bewilderment.

*'Ah so....*we have close connections with Beijing especially in this situation. The first thing the authorities would be afraid of is that it might spread to the provinces so they would take *the* certain precautions. This would include isolating and *containment* of the foreigners because they believe that foreign elements may be promoting these reactionary ideas. No doubt Mr Wu's speech was for this reason. But don't worry,' Chi reassured, reaching tenderly for my hand and

putting an arm around Julie's shoulder. 'These measures may seem harsh now but in a way it is a good thing because it will help to protect you also. The authorities will make sure you are not involved so therefore they won't be able to point the finger at you in any way. Just do as they say and it will be all right. But don't be surprised if we don't have some interesting days ahead.'

'What do you mean Chi, exactly?'

'Well, I think this is only the beginning of great changes in our Chila and I think we will all be affected'

Chi's prediction unfolds like a biblical prophecy. The comfort we absorbed from the warmth of the tea and his caring was too soon dissolved. That evening as we cycle through the college entrance we notice a large group have assembled at the general noticeboard. There was a lot of chatter and discussion going on about the poster that had been put up. It was written in large grass or running style calligraphy - the most individual type of script. Since our knowledge of Chinese decorative handwriting was still primitive we asked one of the students who we recognised, Fang Yuan, to translate. Slowly and painstakingly he explains;

'It is *a praise* of Hu Yao Bong for his service to his country and his high principles, ...most especially his support for free speech and democracy. .....It calls the students to follow their comrades in Beijing ....and gather in mourning at Lanyuan Square...... to protest the cuts in education and government spending, rising inflation, lack of free speech and official corruption.'

Observing the excitement and enthusiasm of the crowds I remark, ' Well it looks like most of the students here will be going.'

'Yes,' says Fang Yuan, 'but not me. I am older than these students and I remember the demonstrations during the Great Cultural Revolution.' The students became out of control then, they took the law into their own hands as you say in English.

Many intellectuals were tortured and beaten and even killed. Anything old was destroyed, including antiques, old buildings, monasteries. So too was anything foreign - so we couldn't learn foreign languages or listen to foreign music. Intellectuals, including students, were considered reactionaries and many were sent to the countryside for re-education. Forced to work like peasants in the fields because Mao feared them and wanted to control them. I was one of those students and I suffered a lot. Not only did I miss on my education but I got very ill. It was very cold in the northern province where I was posted and I didn't have warm enough clothes. I got pneumonia and I nearly died only for the kindness of the farmer I worked with. Even today though my lungs are very weak.

As he spoke I realised that I knew all along in an unconscious way that he was very frail - he was pale and there was a breathlessness in his talk. And for the second time that day I felt a sense of foreboding about the recent twist of events. Although I felt at empathy with what the students were seeking to change I began to see that these demands would not be conceded easily by the authorities and that perhaps the students way of achieving them may not bring justice for all. The age old political questions seemed to forever recur. Does the end justify the means? Does revolutionary change, by it's nature sudden and often violent, preclude a just solution? Can the inexperienced idealism of youth dictate the political history of a nation? Does, as Yeats put it so poignantly, 'too much sacrifice make a stone of the heart?' Can idealism blind our humanity ? How far would the students go to achieve their aims and even more ominously were there political forces within the politburo inciting the students and engineering these changes to their own advantage like Mao did during the Cultural Revolution?

Right now the students were bent on finding their own answers to these questions. They cackled and flocked like wild birds around the posters and up from the crowd came the shout;

'Let's support our comrades in Beijing, let's go to the square now!'

'Yes, yes,' cried the others. 'Down with corruption! Up with democracy! Let's go to the square now!'

The clamour of slogans continued until the group became a common voice of chanting making its way to the dormitory buildings. There they split at the main entrance into smaller groups to be seen again as silhouettes in the faint glow of single light bulbs dangling from the dormitory ceilings. Heads like dark bobbins on a sewing machine encircle the light and suck it and the students out into the night. The groups met again at the college roundabout and made their way to the gate, like wasps swarming.

There as if on queue city buses and xiao mian bao (small white bread as mini buses were called) awaited the students who piled into them with shouts and chants of demonstration. Vacuumed into the whirlwind of this powerful moment of expression of personal political power I found myself following them with the compulsion of one hypnotised.

Julie grabbed me and shaking me out of my spell she yelled,

'No, no.......remember what Chi said.... we are not to get involved. The authorities are watching our every move. It's too dangerous to risk now'

'Of course, you're right,' I apologised though still stunned, 'we'll live to protest another day.'

Little did we realise how soon that day would come upon us and how far away it would make the early days appear.

Chapter Thirteen: In the eye of the Typhoon – a deportee.

'You'll have to get on the next plane out of Lanyuan. The Chinese authorities want you out because of your connection with Chi Hai O.'

The voice on the phone was that of Sean Mc Mahon, the Third Secretary with the Irish Embassy in Beijing. He sounded extremely anxious.

'In fact we are ordering all Irish citizens out because there is an imminent threat of all out civil war. The tanks are firing in at the Embassy compound here in Beijing. The situation is very dangerous. Unfortunately I can't go until all Irish citizens have been evacuated. You are the last person I have to contact. So for my sake if not for your own please leave immediately. I have been trying to contact you for days and so has your family. The communication lines have been severly disrupted by the strike.'

'Yes I know. DWA haven't been able to get through to us either. They contacted one teacher in the Medical College to tell us we had to leave or they would wash their hands of us She has just been here to inform us. But she is refusing to leave. She wants to stay and help with the International Red Cross.'

'Never mind what she or your other colleague is doing it is imperative you get out because of your connection with Chi Hai O. If you stay you could be taken into police custody and it would be difficult for us to get access to you.'

'It's OK..... I realise I must go. I can do nothing for Chi here in China.

Thank you for your concern and help. What part of Ireland are you from by the way?'

'County Clare... just across the water from you'

'Hope to see you there some day then.'

'For sure.. bye for now and you've got my number in case you have any problems getting out. '

'I do and thanks a million.' And a warm sensation of comfort settles in my heart that a complete stranger is concerned and working for my safety. The Irish Embassies have a justified reputation of looking after Irish nationals abroad. Julie has just let Mr Lee from Foreign Affairs into the living room.

His face has no trace of his customary smile.

'We have instructions from the Chinese authorities for Kayleigh to leave immediately and DWA has requested you both to leave straight away. They will pay for your tickets. Our office can get you on the next flight out of Lanyuan.

Please pack all your stuff immediately.

The Americans downstairs are also leaving. There should be a flight this afternoon if it does not rain.'

Seemingly the rain affects flights out of the mountainous regions of China. It is said they don't have proper radar.

Ming Wei and Mei Juan take advantage of the open door and are in to offer their assistance to pack. Luckily I have only the one suitcase. Julie has two. Still I find I am too overcome by savage, conflicting emotions to pack. Ming is doing it for me and I don't care what way the stuff goes in.

I keep trying to focus my mind on what is happening,

trying to make some sense of the events,

trying to stay calm in the midst of the typhoon,

trying not to worry too much about Chi,

trying to follow the Tao and remain centred

breathing deeply into my solar plexus as I had been trained. It's too difficult.

'The many gifts given by the students will have to be packed separately.' Ming is saying.

'Yes, of course' I was agreeing with her in English and Chinese... just agreeing with anything she said. Ming's directedness was a comfort to me.

The students had begun to arrive to say good bye, another welcome distraction. Mr Yang and Yu Chin were the first. I had given then extra help to prepare for the TOEFL exam for which they were grateful beyond my due. It had been no bother, they were such dedicated and polite students, they were a pleasure to share knowledge with. I thought I was going to surely cry then when I saw in their faces the fear that with the foreign teachers gone all hopes of ever travelling *to abroad* were going with our plane. All hopes of a modern and advanced China open to the world of new ideas dashed.

I told them not to worry I'd be back, we'd all be back. This was just a temporary setback.

They smiled and shook hands, thanked me for everything and said they hoped I was right. They had some gifts. From Mr Yang; Chinese enamel chopsticks with a neat inscription of thanks and devotion to his foreign teacher on the inside of the box. From Yu Chin; an ancient Chinese coin with a whole through its centre to thread it on a string. The box also had a sentimental message.

'To teacher Kayleigh No matter how far apart we will always be friends - good friends never forget each other. Yu Chin.'

I was on the verge of tears but I managed to keep face after all these months of practice. Still I knew my eyes betrayed my emotion just as theirs did theirs.

Alice and Marie popped their two lovely lantern-like heads in the door. They were always a delight to see but especially now in such bleak times. Their two, youthful, intelligent and optimistic faces represented to me all that was possible for the new China. They had fallen so in love with their English names. They always used them with us. They were English teachers but wanted to become interpreters or work with an international company. They refused to believe we wouldn't be back but had brought gifts to make sure we did not forget.

One of a porcelain couple kissing, representing my future marriage. And inscribed in the box; 'To my darling Kayleigh.

May you marry soon, be very happy and have many *of* children.'

Another was a silk scroll in Chinese running style calligraphy with the Chinese characters for forbearance, a heart with a knife held above it. I told Marie I would carry it close to my heart on the journey.

Between Julie's and my students the room was a buzz of farewells. The retinue at the door continued until it was time to go to the airport. Many said they would accompany us, either on the college bus or by private bus. Luckily the road to the airport was in a westerly direction out of the city and was not blockaded.

And so we left Lanyuan on a dismal day - overcast like our minds - grey bleak like our mood. The airport enclosed us further in our melancholy but made our group even more united. A number of students were crying. It was an uncharacteristic display of emotion.

They all looked forlorn.

'Please don't forget us' they pleaded.

'Pleased don't forget us.' they wept.

'You must tell the world what is happening here. Don't let the world forget what happened here'

Mr (Fat) Wu, the Dean, looked as indifferent as ever, but maybe not, who ever knew how he felt, how anyone felt.

Mr Lee looked genuinely upset.

'The saddest send off we have given any foreign teachers.' he said.

'Because this sending off is the sending off of our hopes and dreams. Will the expulsion of foreigners lead to the closing up of China - the raising again of the bamboo curtain?'

'I feel guilty for leaving you all. I feel like I am deserting you, especially Chi.' I could feel my voice waiver.

'Its not your fault.' says Mr Lee with the assurance of a father consoling a child. 'There is no other way. Don't worry we will try our best to get Chi released as soon as possible. There must be some mistake. You are better to him in Ireland for now. Take it up with you own Government.'

'At least I know all of you will be safe.' I feel I have lost connection with my own voice as it takes on an unfamiliar high pitch.

'Yes we will. Our students were not involved in any serious way in any of the demonstrations so do not worry.' Mr Lee's voice is by contrast to mine as confident as a spring stream. His precious experience of upheaval has strengthened his character.

We all shook hands and even took mutual photos but it was a very subdued

sad

sad

send off.

As the plane swung into the air I thought I'm looking my last on Lanyuan and my eyes lovingly surveyed its moonscape loess mountains and irrigated valleys and prayed for a happy end to the turmoil.

Southwards to Guangzhou into the lush green and steam of the subtropics.

What are we to face here?

By all accounts Guanzhou is in a state of siege too. Transportation is severely restricted. Luckily we have only to travel within the airport. Julie is in no mood for talking so I will take the opportunity to find my centre again in the quietness of meditation in order to remain calm yet alert in this time of crisis.

But my meditation is naturally not as peaceful as usual. Other thoughts start to penetrate the quiet and even though I try to ignore them they remain. My mind keeps filing through the sequence of events that have led to this - fleeing China.

We had several warning that the Government were going to clampdown. External warnings from the Government and internal omens from the landscape of the psyche - our own intuition.

The most scary foreboding of the eventual turmoil came to me in the form of a dream, some nights ago.

In the dream I was lying on a mattress on the floor in a room with no other furniture except a fan overhead. The fan is whirring round at a medium speed but suddenly it starts to fly at a fantastic rate. As it does the wings of the fan turn into giant crab claws flying around faster and faster. They take off from their hold in the ceiling and whirr around uncontrollably closing in on me. The picture shifts. Now I am in the neighbouring room lying on a mattress on the floor. A man, Chi, is sleeping on my left. No words are spoken but Chi signals for me to check the room for myself. I know I must go into the room on my own. A giant crab lays dead on the floor the claws have left dark red blood stains on the wall.

At eight o'clock the following morning there is a strong knock on the door. I open it to find Fang Yuan looking pale and haggard.

'What's wrong?'

'It's Chi they have taken him.'

'Who's taken him? What?' I scream as I feel my heart beat roller coaster out of control.

'The Secret police came to his rooms in the college last night.'

'But where have they taken him?'

'We don't know... that's the trouble with the secret police... he could be anywhere.'

'Do his parents know?'

'Yes and the college authorities ....they are doing everything to find him.'

'Oh, my God and I clutch the handle of the door.'

Fang puts his arm around me, steadies me in the door and seats me on the nearby armchair.

Julie is in the hallway asking questions

My mind goes into a spin. 'I can't seem to grasp what herself and Fang are saying. The whole room goes into a spin and the next thing I know I am lying on my bed looking at Julie, bent prostrate over me giving me some water.

'It's all right.' she is saying. ' You passed out with shock.'

'Chi, where is Chi?' I moan. 'What have they done to him?'

'He'll be all right. He's done nothing serious. Don't you worry now'

'Dr. Yang is giving you an injection for shock.'

'No. no I don't want an injection I want to go find him.'

and I try to struggle out of bed but I am held down by Julie's strong arm and I feel the nip in my upper thigh.

'That's what we were afraid you might do,' says Julie firmly, ' go looking for him... that would be too dangerous for both of you. Fang is doing all he can. So are the college. The Dean has a lot of clout. Even Rose Bray has the Red Cross looking into it.'

Julie's voice begins to fade into the distance as the effects of the sedative swamps my system.

Before I open my eyes the next morning I steer my consciousness into my meditation despite the sedation. My Third Eye intuition tells me that Chi's arrest was part of the Governments reaction to the mounting pressure being exerted on them. It was only a matter of time before force would be used in Tiananmen Square if not all over China.

The students had become more confident, more entrenched in their demands. They wanted the government to speak to their elected representatives not those appointed by the Government. Gorbachev was coming to China. How could the government tolerate this show of dissent? As negotiations failed the government had given their ultimatum to the students; they would occupy the square.

Sure enough the Government fulfilled its promise.

That night.

I remember well.

It started to rain.

The first rain we had since April.

Julie and I, we were walking back from one of the teachers house's after watching TV. The first omen; the Public Address system was taken over again by the authorities.

The voice was forceful, dictatorial, Orwellian. We understood the message.

'The Government will take control of Tiananmen square from the counter revolutionaries and criminals who are occupying it illegally. All those illegally occupying the square leave immediately. All means necessary will be used.'

The students had been ordered out of the square before. The tanks had been ordered in. But each time they had been sent back. Overnight ordinary people had become heroes. They had held back the Chinese army by peaceful protest. They walked out in front of the tanks and asked the Peoples' army not to shoot the people. The Peoples army retreated. There were scenes of soldiers being embraced by the people. Of soldiers embracing the people. It was a triumph for humanity. It was the very best of being human.

This time it was different.

This time it wasn't the Peoples Liberation Army that had been sent in. They were special combat forces withdrawn from the Mongolian border. It was rumoured

that they were on adrenaline-type drugs. They were brainwashed that they were facing anti-government forces in the square, not students but counter-revolutionaries, terrorists and common criminals.

The death toll was uncertain. Figures between hundreds and thousands. Who will ever know except the families and loved ones of those no longer here.

On the plane again I am looking over my dairies, a futile attempt to make sense of the jumble of life, to come to terms with what is happening, why it is happening.

It was all supposed to have started on Qing Ming Jie on April the 14th. That was the day the Huo Yao Beng died, but did it? When does anything ever begin?

Qing Ming Jie in Chinese is the festival of *clear*

brightness. It is the time to worship the ancestors by visiting their graves and tidying and refurbishing them *(the Grave Sweeping Festival)*. Ancestor worship is one of the ancient Chinese religions and this is one of the major ways it has survived. It is celebrated on the 4th. and 5th. of April, fixed dates based on the solar agricultural calendar. Signs of the festival had been apparent for weeks on the streets of Lanyuan.

Multicoloured funeral wreaths made of paper flowers in all sizes to the gigantic were being sold from pavement stalls and shops. In the markets street hawkers were cajoling passers-by to buy josh sticks and yellow paper money. People believe that by burning this paper money they will send it to their forefathers in the after life ensuring their wealth and safe passage to the other side.

Chi invited myself and Julie to his family's yearly visit to Zhu Hua Shan, the mountain where his fathers cremated body lay. We were joined by his mother and sisters, uncle aunt and two nephews. At the foot of the mountain some magical old women were selling the traditional funeral wares. They were of a Muslim minority, Hui Ming, dressed in black and wearing a veil type white head dress. Their expressions belied the passage of history and their eyes had the sparkle of foresight but they refused our cameras as wisdom perpetually evades youth and naiveté

As is often the case with Chinese holy mountains the climber is denied the adventure of the slippery slope by stone paved steps. Perched in squatting position along the route were vendors of edibles and potables; beef noodles and water melon seeds, fizzy drinks, Chinese spirits and beer.

Chi's arm extended to aid his mother. I followed, chatting to his sister, Lin, who spoke English. At the end of the steps the path became dusty, winding its way through the redbrick and mud huts of the community who balanced delicately on the hillside.

The path ends in a plateau with an alter embedded into the

mountain side. The alter is divided up into glass orifices from which the milling throngs are taking urns and placing them on nearby wooden or stone tables and gathering around to worship. Chi has the key to his fathers shrine and we follow his mother to the nearest resting place, a grassy spot on the plateau. We are all encouraged to squat around.

Chi talks to his fathers urn in Chinese as does his mother and the rest of the relatives. Apart from his mothers wet eyes there is no other visible signs of emotion but the voices are gentle warm and coaxing.

I ask Lin about her father.

'Your father died very young, didn't he?'

'Yes.. he was only fifty-five. During the Cultural Revolution he was beaten badly by a group of students from the Red Guard for being an intellectual..... one of the despised classes. Then he was sent for re-eductaion to the countryside. Conditions were very bad and his lungs were damaged by pneumonia. When he came back to teach at the University when the Cultural Revolution was over his health never improved. He died of a heart attack in 1980.'

'I'm so sorry.... you must have been very young.'

'I was only ten, Chi was fifteen. He was very kind and knowledgeable. We miss him a lot. Mother says Chi is like him in many ways, even in appearance.'

'Then he must have been handsome.'

'Yes as you English say tall, dark and handsome. How I wish he were here today but at least I know he is here in spirit along with the spirit of all our ancestors and all those who died as a result of the Great Cultural Revolution. I hope nothing like that ever happens again.'

'I'm sure it won't when a country has one bad experience like that I don't think it's quick to repeat. We had a civil war in Ireland in the 1920's and we look back on that time with deep regret. A country learns from its mistakes just as a person does.'

'I hope you are right.' Lin's face takes on the aspect of

Rita Hogan

someone older than her years.

'Hey you two,' shouts Chi, ' what are you looking so serious about?'

'Come and join us in a toast.' and he hands us two glasses of baijui.

'Long may we connect to our past lives in the present and look forward to our future. *Dry glass.*' and everyone downs their drinks. Chi fills them up again.

'Long may we have the company of foreign friends, especially my dear Kayleigh. *Dry glass'*

'To your family and to our friendship. *Dry glass'* I rejoin with a smile. We polish off our glasses again. Then Chi turns to me and says, 'You have been missing out on the beer. Let us get you in the merry mood of Chinese ancestor worship. When we celebrate here our forebears are joining in their world beyond the skies.'

'You mean there is alcohol in Chinese heaven?'

'Oh yes... lots of it but the kind of stuff that does not make you *mao lao*.... old head....how do you say in English? '

'You mean drunk, I think?'

'And the next day you feel good too.'

'Oh no hangover...... that seems heavenly all right..... tell me more.'

'Aye ya, Chinese heaven is the kind of place where you can experience love without jealousy, joy without pain, friendship without competition, happiness without sorrow knowledge without ignorance, faith without doubt, courage without fear. Where the union of opposites gives rise to eternal good.'

'Sounds very abstract, Chi, but what does it mean in practice? Love without jealousy would that mean you wouldn't be jealous of any of my previous boyfriends.' I tease.

'Exactly... they would have their place in your life in the past and would be seen as such. But there would be no jealousy on my part. Just understanding and love.'

'So could people have affairs then and their partners would not get jealous?'

'Aye ya.. I think you joke with me. There would only be a relationship between two people because there would be no need for affairs as each would find his perfect partner.'

'But what if you died at the age of ninety without a partner?'

'Of course you would become youthful again and there your perfect partner would be waiting for you.'

'In that case I think I'll nod off now and get a one way ticket there.'

'No.. no.. that's the thing you cannot get there until you've earned the price of the ticket in this life first.'

'But what if I die before I earned it?'

'You die and go to the middle world for a while until you reincarnate and get a chance to be human again and then find heaven.'

'Oh that's a bit more complicated than I thought. Then I think I'll stick it out here for a while longer and try to get it right the first time'

'Oh no this is not your first time here. You are an old soul'

'What do you mean....an old soul?'

'You have been through many reincarnations. We have met before.'

And he gave me that all-knowing smile of an ancient Buddha and my heart began to resonate in a dancing rhythm.

This man could convince me of anything, I thought, and I seem incapable of watching my feet stepping not to mind stopping them step into his world.

It wasn't until the next day that we found out that Hu Yao Beng was dead and that there had been demonstrations in Beijing. Mr Wu gave myself and Julie the lecture about our classes. After that day events took on a roller coaster momentum. The entire college was out on strike by the first of May. Rumour had it so was the rest of Lanyuan and all the major cities. The countryside, where the majority of the population still dwelt, remained unaffected. The farmers had done particularly well under the new reforms. Agricultural production had improved and they were able to sell their surplus at market rates and improve their standard of living.

Chi called to my room early on May Day morning. Normal college life was at a standstill. Even the reception personnel at the You Yi Bing Yuan, our Foreign Guest House, were not on duty. Since the telling off by Mr Wu the reception had been given instructions to check all visitors who came to see us by asking for their identity cards and writing their names into a visitor's book. They were obviously no longer interested in our activities. The larger picture was now dominating their lives.

Chi was very excited. It was the first time I'd seen him flushed.

'Hey what about your Taoist training now? I joked. 'Remain calm in the storm.'

'One must also go in accordance with the forces of nature. When action is called for one must act.'

'Come,' he said urgently, 'there's a truck waiting outside with my Art College students and colleagues.'

'Can I bring a camera?'

'Yes.. everyone has cameras.'

As we hurried along the broad avenue sheltered by the ripening leaves of spring we were joined by colourful throngs of singing students and teachers in their spring colours waving vibrant banners with daring slogans.

Carnival was in the air. The atmosphere felt more like a Saint Patrick's Day parade in New York than a demonstration. Many were in costume. More wore bandannas of red across their shiny black hair, sporting white tee-shirts with slogans for democracy brandished across them. They had drums and pipes and they were cheering and singing. Outside the college gates military style trucks converted for commercial use and now political purpose waited to hoard the swarming crowds onto their flatbacks, standing as many as fifty to a truck.

All day to day traffic was at a standstill. All public transport was being put to the service of the demonstrations.

To the sides of the main boulevards in the special bicycle lanes the cyclists were also parading in style, blazing white banners and singing as they made their way down Mian Lu, the winding river road running between the purple mountains.

Congestion was widespread at cross-roads where bands of protesters joined up accidentally or by design to swell into a much larger hoard of bobbing black spools of heads making their way to the square. On the way they were cheered and encouraged by shopkeepers, passers-by and residents, giving out free drinks and food and lending words of praise and encouragement.

Some shops had large pictures of Mao and Zhou En Lai. There were posters saying how both leaders had remained honest and loyal to the people to the end. I had a deep sense of foreboding about this. The last time there were posters of Mao on widespread display in China was during the Cultural Revolution. But Chi said it was a very different type of protest in a different era; a protest for freedom rather than oppression, a demonstration for human rights rather than against them.

The square was thronged with students and banners and posters of protest. Buses were converted to housing around the centre stage where rallying speeches were being voiced amid cheers, often bursting into song and music. All sections of society were represented; many came to demonstrate their support for the cause, others came out of curiosity. An old lady dressed in a navy blue tunic and pants perched on tiny (previously-bound?) feet squeezed up against us in the crowd and turned her grandchild to have a look at the foreigner. The year-old child, grabbed my hair, gurgled and said,

'Nai Nai.'

Chi and the old woman laughed.

'She thinks you are her grandmother because of your light coloured hair.' The child and I were laughing and fondling each other when Fang Yuan appeared out of nowhere and whispered something to Chi.

Chi's look changed from one of cheer to one of worry.

'There's a man over there taking photos of you. Fang doesn't think he is a civilian. The camera looks like a professional one. I think we must *to* go.'

'That's all right I'll go back on my own.' I insist. 'It's best you are not seen with me.'

But Chi is also insistent.

'That's no problem. Come on let us get out of here fast.'

But Fang is thinking for both of us.

'Chi maybe its best you stay to make your speech. I'll go back with Kayleigh.'

'Well I suppose I can trust you to take her home safely. Chi jibes and squeezes my hand goodbye.

'You know she will be fine.' Fang smiles. 'Come along Kayleigh. The man is still taking photographs.'

Luckily we are travelling on foot and by bike. No car would have made it through the crowds. It was the second time that day my exuberance had been chilled by sinister foreboding but I said nothing to Fang Yuan on the cycle home as I didn't wish to dampen his enthusiasm. He seemed unusually optimistic. Maybe he was thinking of going abroad again. If China became more open and democratic he wouldn't need to marry to do so.

More dairy entries- three days later.

Third of May.

I am in Chi's' home, sipping tea and eating watermelon seeds, listening comfortably almost casually, to a student Government Press conference. As if it was the natural order of things for a group of powerless students to make demands on one of the most powerful oligarchies in the world, supported as it was by the military might of the Chinese army.

The students demand that the Government meet with representatives from the demonstrations and not the Beijing Student Federation, which is a Government elected body.

They demand to be given equal status in negotiations with the Government.

They request that representatives from the National Political Council and standing members of the politburo be present at negotiations.

The students pledge to continue their demonstrations if the Government does not respond.

The Government appear to be responding respectfully to the student challenge. They are very measured and reasonable in their dialogue. They say they have no doubt about the students patriotism. They even agree with the students that there are problems with corruption and embezzlement and would like to work with the students to promote democracy and deepen reform.

However they calmly advise the students to return to class to restore order to the cities and not to follow the instruction of those who only wish to create disorder and unrest. They warn the students that if they violate the criminal code they will be arrested.

International interest in the demonstrations has increased. On the radio, The BBC World Service and the Voice of America give blow by blow accounts of events in the square. The students and teachers are glued to them both though most people consider the BBC more objective. The TV cameras are there too - from all over the world. We wonder how long will the Government tolerate the International media. Fang Li Zhi, a leading dissident and respected professor, suggests US business boycott China because of Human rights violations. Fang Li Zhi founded the China Democratic League based in the USA which has been declared illegal by the Chinese Government.

Eight of May.

Mr Wu comes to the apartment to tell Julie and I he will no longer be our Chinese teacher. We wonder is he trying to distance himself from us because we are foreigners and it might go against him in case of a crackdown. Or is he afraid for being accused of corruption for taking our classes in the first place when he wasn't qualified to do so.

Twelfth of May.

The party leadership, despite the rhetoric, have not responded to the students demands. The students in Beijing go on hunger strike. The students in Lanyuan go on strike in sympathy. So too do the students in the other cities. The students take over the Public Address system in the colleges and we now get a view of the protests from the student perspective. Julie and I are asked to the College Communications Tower to translate what is going on in Beijing from CNN, the American TV network. The students have lost faith in the Chinese TV accounts and only listen to it for clues as to what way the leadership may be going.

Rumours along the railway lines that Deng Xiao Peng has been shot by a body guard.

Thirteenth of May.

It is rumoured Deng has survived the attack on his life. There are further rumours that there is a power struggle within the party and that the different leaders are going to the seven military strongholds, including Lanyuan, to drum up support from the army. The PLA seems to have become the most important player.

Nineteenth of May.

CCTV announces that the students have given up their hunger strike. This is not true.

Martial law is declared in all major cities.

The dairies have become skint. The details have been taken

over by events. My personal account has been superseded by history.

.

Today is the fifth of June. The day after the troops moved into the square. Two days after Chi's arrest. I am flying into Guanzhou. It is surprisingly easy to get a ticket to Hong Kong at the international airport. We, a motley crew of foreigners, only have to wait a couple of hours to be hurled by the typhoon into calm at its centre and to relative safety.

Safety is a relative thing. The hungry hounds of the International Press are there to meet us on arrival at Kai Tak airport. Their appetite for news of China is voracious. We are the first foreigners out of the provinces. They jostle with each other to get close to us. They have microphones in their hands. It's like seeing people being hounded by the Press on TV except you are those people. One particular monster heaves his breathless microphone into my face and shouts;

'Did you see anyone die? Were there any of your students shot?'

'No, no.. please can I get by. I'm too tired to talk now.'

I rush for shelter behind a burly DWA representative who I recognise from my orientation. DWA arrange for interviews tomorrow afternoon with the papers Julie and I have selected on grounds of objectivity and sincerity.

Even though I will have time to prepare and I know these newspapers have integrity I am still worried if I am doing the right thing.

Will it only incense the Government more against Chi and the other students if pressure is put on them by the press? They do not have much respect for the International press in the first place and the Chinese Government do not like having their backs put up against the wall by anyone.

Who should we meet up with for dinner that evening but Ole Rupert. He wasn't going to wait for the rest of the volunteers in the provinces to leave before he got out, now was he? Not the same calibre as the Irish Embassy man, by any means. I am almost glad to see him despite the woodeness of his personality hidden behind his suit of Oxbridge manners.

Maybe events will return to a cyclical continuity after all, maybe the circle will be completed. I met him at the beginning now comfortingly he is here at the end.

'I am quite adamant that it is a good i*dear* to meet with the members of the press.'

Rupert is proselytising over a full glass of Burgundy. The British and American governments have already pledged support for the students and offered asylum to the leaders. Even if they do not fulfil this promise they will put pressure on the Chinese Government for their release, particularly those who have received media attention. Don't worry your Chi will be out in no time. The press will adore your story. The romance of it.'

Rupert was right . The press did like the story. So much so that even though I had only given details to a few select papers with integrity the tabloids got hold of it and it was headlines;

Irish Girl's Romance in Tiananmen Square.
Tiananmen student leader has Irish love.

There was no knowing what path our story would take now that the media had taken part ownership.

Chapter Fourteen: Chi's escapade

Lao Yu was standing before him in the guise of an old woman. Yet he recognised the voice and felt the familiarity of her energy.

'I'm sorry you had to endure so long but my contact with the Spirit World advised that it was necessary to increase your strength of mind, to prove your devotion to the pathway, your understanding of its meaning.'

'Yes I can see it was necessary. I was too impulsive, too passionate before now. I didn't have the centredness or understanding.'

Lao Yu's eyes penetrate deep into Chi's, as if she is looking into his soul.

'Yes indeed you have changed. Now you can understand that I have cast a sleeping spell over the whole prison community - a kind of magic manipulation of the natural which before now you were unable to accept. When they wake up you will be dead. Except the body they will find will be mine not yours. I will have shape-changed into your body as my Taoist alchemical powers allow. But I can move out of that body at will and take another form. When they cremate me my spirit will fly into the body of an eagle due to fly over at precisely the right time. You will remain in your body. With a little magic we will add a beard, give you a sun tan, and the clothing of a monk.

'Yes now I understand the circumstances in which it is right to use such supernatural powers.' Chi stands still, returning her gaze.

'Which is why we have chosen you and Kayleigh to be among those to spread the Way to the West. Both of you are dominated by the way of love and will only use your powers in the correct manner. It is essential that the Tao be taught in this way, guided by the princples of love and rightness. And now to deal with the practical things; here is some Yuan. You will make your way by this compass, going directly west to the Magi caves. There a monk, Lao San, will be waiting for you with further instructions. Go now and to anyone who stops you these are your papers.

You are now the fully fledged Taoist monk, Xiao Ming - *Little Bright One-*

Go Xiao Ming.

Do not dither.

The spell will be wearing off soon.'

And as she gives him the formal *wai*, the joining of hands in the Eastern form of prayer and the bowing of the head, there are tears in her eyes.

This is a sign of her tribute to him, of their equality.

He returned the *wai* and thanked her.

She put her hand on his shoulder and signalled him off.

Just as he was exiting the prison gates a guard wakes up and chases after him.

Chi continues in haste.

'Stop or I will fire.'

Chi turns towards him

'I have my hands up. Please don't shoot'

and he recognises the face of his chief interrogator.

'I see we are to dual it out to the last. I knew you would ignore my reports of your non-repentance. I could have increased your sentence to a lifetime in prison. You wouldn't even help me by pretending to have recanted. What was I to do? You put me in an abominable position.'

His gun was down by his side now. His expression almost entreating.

'You could have played the game like others before you have - pretended to be a converted communist. I didn't want to make those reports but you would not co-operate why not..... why not? and his voice rose to a high pitch beseeching prayer of a question.

'I think you know in your inner self why. That we cannot live our life as a lie. If we do that's what we become – a lie. Even the pretence of collaboration is conceding your own power to the authorities. If I was to pretend to collaborate who would know the difference on the outside? I would after all follow through with the pretence and loose my self respect and dignity among my comrades. Is this what you really want? A society of fear where everyone is afraid to reveal his heart to the other? Is this what you want for your country? Is this what any patriot would want for his country? Tell me that it is and I will tell you that it is not the way of the Tao, the way of the ancestors, the way of the true Descendants of the Dragon. The only way forward for our country is truth; the only road is the road of integrity and sincerity. We can neither hide it or corrupt it or kill it because truth has a way of showing up in the most unlikeliest of corners; in the eyes of a new born baby who will mock your lies, in the smile of a true love which would shame your mendacity, in a colleague whose warmth scorns your lack of sincerity.'

Chi realises he is preaching but he knows the time is ripe to continue as Guo Le is entranced and receptive to every word.

'Because the only way forward for us Chinese is the ancient and eternal way of the Tao followed by the Chinese people throughout the ages despite political upheaval through different empires and regimes. Our leaders know this in their hearts even if they do not express it to the people. An unjust leader does not have the authority vested in him by the people and he will eventually loose his power. As stated in the ancient book of Chinese wisdom the I Ching. *The people cannot be ruled by coercion and by force but by guidance and advice.* Do you believe this Guo le?'

Gou Le's outstretched arm trembles and shakes and he drops the gun which tumbles to the ground.

'Of course in my heart I believe this but in these times there seems to be no way out.'

'There is always a way Guo Le, even if the way is obscure at first. As we travel it becomes clear - the fog dissolves and the sun shines through. This is the natural way of things between heaven and earth and beyond to the source of all things, the Tao.'

Chi moves towards him as he utters these words and pulling him to his feet says;

'Do not feel overburdened by the times. Things are changing. There are many more like me and even more like you who are just beginning to feel the re-awakening. Do not fear. Nothing will be asked of you of which you are not capable and you will not have to endure hardships beyond your endurance. Your role will become clearer to you and you will act when the time is ripe for action. What you have seen here today will remain with you for it is no illusion. You have seen the sorceress's magic because it had to be made manifest for you to believe. You will not flinch from your future now. Your destiny will be clear to you.'

'But what will happen when everyone wakes up and finds you no longer here. For sure I will be blamed.' Guo Le's face is stricken grey by fear.

'All that's been taken care of too as you will soon see. Let the passage of earthly time perform its natural function.' With these words Chi radiated green healing light from his Third Eye to assuage and strengthen Gou Le. The light achieved its purpose and Guo Le responded;.

'I am still afraid of what is to come but some how I trust what you say. Thank you my friend for taking the time to introduce me to the path. I am forever in your debt.' And Guo le hugged Chi with the familiarity and warmth of a close brother.

'There are no debts owed my friend. The favour has been returned. I must go quickly as the spell will son dispel.'

Chi ran down the pathway through the iron gateway left unlocked by the still slumbering guards. It would be a while

before he reached the nearest village which he knew to be ten
li ahead but he didn't find the journey arduous. He found
himself running madly in stages and then dancing sprightly
and hopping and skipping and whistling at the top of his
voice. It was a desolate mountain area and he felt secure he
was not being watched

Chi's words;
By the time I reach the village it is dusk. In such a remote
area there won't be a guesthouse but if I offer money a room
would be found. I find a shop front at the side of the road. It is
a home converted into a store. Most of the items for sale are
piled up high on a table on the roadside; cans of fruit and
vegetables, crates of soda making a colourful display. The old
woman behind the table is chomping on a cigarette in a mouth
that reveals few teeth.

'What do you want she asked in gruff country tones, not
meaning to sound unfriendly.

'Any fruit left, mother?' she points to some crab apples in a
torn bamboo basket.

'I'll have a bag full and some of that sweet bread.'

'That will be two Yuan,' she says with the slight flicker of
an eye which in our culture denoted deceit.'

I didn't think she'd try to overcharge a monk but you can
always fool an outsider and on outsider is always an outsider

Just to let her know that I know I say,

'Apples are expensive this time of year how much would a
bed be going for?'

'How many nights?'

'One at the most.'

'I can give you a huan of your own for five Yuan.'

'Three would suit me better.'

'Four and your done.'

'An Mei,' she shouts in through the doorway. The sound of
scuttling feet comes nearer and a shy teenager responds.

'Yes mother.'

'Can you show the monk a room, your older brother's room will do...And show him where the outside toilet is.'

The next thing I remember is been woken out of the depths by the cocks before dawn and the howling of the dogs following quickly after. Sheer exhaustion had overcome my fear of discovery.

I was completely confident with Lao Yu's magic powers. I understood the spell merely transported the occupants of the prison out of the current time space dimension into the fourth dimension where space and time stand still. When they returned to the three-dimensional reality they would not have a memory of it and no side effects. It will be business as usual at the camp except for the death of a young Taoist artist and counter-revolutionary. The death itself would require explanation. They would probably apply the usual prison cause, pneumonia.

But amongst the officials themselves it was bound to cause some consternation.

There had been no signs of previous illness.

Had he willed himself to death rather than capitulate? they secretly thought to themselves. There was a smile on his face and his body had no marks but something about my dead body caused an unease that swept from one official to the other across the prison camp. Officialdom always requires an explanation a specific cause of death and now in fact there was none

I can see them in the office; the three Chiefs of Staff working together on that report. The looks between them - the sweat from at least one brow. There was an enough superstition in those eyes of converted communists to suspect the causes may have been supernatural.

The Lao Yu School is renowned in China for its powers. There was intense surprise in the first place that one of its members was arrested. But it was for my part in the student revolt and not my Taoist ties. The Government was determined to make an example of anyone who opposed then no matter what their societal standing. Still this was more than the example they would have wanted - a dead man in a prison cell. It was intended to incarcerate him for a year at most during which time he was supposed to confess and repent his actions, and be returned, rehabilitated to the community.

He was to be a lesson to academia and to the Taoist and other religions that political dissent was not the proper course of action. There was one and only one party in China, the Communist party, and that Party was on the right course of action; greater economic freedom without the political freedom which had led to the break-up of the Soviet Union. A strong and united party meant a strong and united China.

The government felt sure that the lesson had been learnt by the taking of the Square by their military forces, squashing the revolt of counter-revolutionaries and common criminals, the arrest and punishment of the ringleaders.

Through my Third Eye I can see;

the supervisor of the prison is chain-smoking as he paces his dingy cold office as cheerless as any of the prison cells. He looks furtively at his inferior officers but no enlightenment seems forthcoming. He has faced worst decisions, greater cover-ups than this, like the deaths of Tibetan monks in the prisons in Gaoling. There the causes were natural but inflicted by men under his supervision. Some of the torture and cruelty had sickened even him. He asked for a transfer later.

But this was a real mystery. Guo Le, the prisoners interrogator seemed to be the key.

'Well Guo Le what have you come up with?'

'I have made a brief preliminary report Sir and attached the opinion of the medical authorities.'

The supervisor peruses through the report.

He looks up and searches Guo Le's eyes.

'So it was you who found him?'

'Yes sir, he failed to show up for afternoon labour. I went looking for him and I found him lying in his cell bed. He was completely still and I could not rouse him so I called the medics. Without an autopsy they say its impossible to identify with certainty the causes of his death but I pressed them for a possible cause and they postulated a blood clot or haemorrhage to the brain which can occur at any time without warning.'

'Well we can't afford an autopsy.... But since there is no sign of injury or mistreatment it will not require great explanation.'

So Lao Yu was right. It would all come to pass with ease. Just like the rest of my journey. Magi Shan is only a jostling bus ride away. The driver turns off the engine going down the hills to save petrol, relying solely on the brakes for control. Not unusual practice in the countryside but nerve-wrecking all the same. Some of the passengers, country people unused to the travel are getting sick up front. Minor obstacles on the path of life.

Lao San is waiting for me with a ticket for the train to Russia. I am travelling as a member of the Lao Yu School to study on exchange in the West. There is already a group in Dublin to await me. Kayleigh knows nothing yet. She thinks I am dead. Lao Yu will inform her by telepathy in the next few days.

The Trans - Mongolian express cuts across Mongolia to Siberia and on to Moscow. From Moscow I fly to Dublin. By that time Kayleigh will know I am on my way.

Kayleigh's Account.

I got word of Chi's death from his mum. The letter was in Chinese characters so I couldn't read it all. I could tell was it was sent by Chi's mother, Mei Ling Hua, I knew those characters well. It was written in red ink. I knew that was a bad omen - the breaking off of relations, finished business. I contacted Wang Kai at the Chinese Cultural Centre he gave me a complete translation.

Chi Hai O has died of natural causes, a blood clot to the brain, while in the custody of the Chinese authorities. The Chinese Government will not give me a visa to enter China for the funeral probably due to my work with Political Prisoners Abroad. Chi is to be cremated at his favourite spot, Wu Tai Shan, one of the main centres of Taoism in China. His mother promised to send me some of his ashes.

A week later the ashes came in tact in a gold gilded funeral vase with Chi's photo in the front. So it was true, it was true, there was no mistake but there must be some mistake.

There are so many people of one surname in China it was estimated there are only one hundred common surnames. With hundreds of thousands in prison there could still be a mistake. But now the photo came and the vase with proof. Either his family had been duped by the government or it was really true. Was it really true?

Lao Yu's visitation came before I had time to descend into despair. She came to me in my dream. She had taught that with practice our whole life would become a meditation. When we work we meditate when we meditate we work. Our life becomes a communion with the whole of life and not the separation we have previously experienced. We become the dancer and the dance. When we first begin to meditate we try to achieve the state of mind of one asleep, unconscious yet aware. Now our sleep becomes, a meditation, a state of enlightened awareness. And in that state, where the brain is receptive to higher vibrations we can communicate on different wave-lengths - at higher levels of consciousness - at psyche levels of communication.

And so Lao Yu was able to appear before me in the liquid light of my dream to tell me what I already knew..... that Chi was still alive. That his family had collaborated with the Government in making believe he was dead. That the two of us were now on a spiritual path together, the path of enlightened love. Our only repayment to the Tao was to live the life of the Tao and by example spread its light. It seemed natural that we would both become involved with Lao Yu's School here in Ireland, the existence of which has only now been revealed to me. It was where our path was taking us. We are after all, we all are, descendants of the path of love.

Epilogue Chapter 15: Return to the now.

Dublin airport baggage control.

Chi's thoughts;

Customs control..... I seem to be going through in a twilight haze. automatically. not thinking. Authority no longer scares me... I've moved beyond that fear. What drives me now is the heat coursing through my veins, a fire lighting up my heart making my consciousness all a twirl with thoughts of her. Will she know me? Will she see the real me despite the physical differences, the lighter skin and eyes, the scar on my chin, the limp?

Will fire be matched by fire, love by love, flame to flame? Molten the liquid in the veins that love only her whose eyes will shortly meet mine. I tremble as if electrified.

Past customs control now the glass exit doors are sliding open as I step on the mat. I breathe fire longing desire. Dare I look up until I have composed myself?

Where is she now?

Eyes floor-bound I feel another heat luring me towards her. I follow meekly I cannot choose, its pull too magnetic to resist, a pathway separate from those in front to a barricade where I find her all aglow with light, angelic warm and waiting.

My bags drop to the floor as we embrace across the barricade the world explodes into fire. Her energy abounding, her skin luminescent, her loving eyes, the softness of her embrace, we are caught in the inferno for a magnetic instant and realise we are being watched.

'Come around follow the crowd' *she beckons. I pick up my bags obediently and follow her around until we can at last embrace fully.*

Kayleigh.

I can't believe it is Chi. I thought too long a wait would make my heart a cold place but no the very opposite it can hardly contain the hot spring of emotion - my blood has become a boiling brew of love. But it's really true. What little difference the vessel of the body makes to the soul.

A slightly darker tinge of colour, extra hair. Oh my God, he's got a scar and a slight limp. Was he badly hurt? My blood stops coursing - stagnant. No. no this is not the Tao of Life. I must flow, follow the movement the course of the river. Dont' stagnate the river with fear. Relax and breathe, he is here, has survived and look has all the previous vibrancy in those eyes.

Those eyes.

Pulling me towards him as the river towards the sea. Come to me come to me my darling here you will find your succour your release. And I am caught in the embrace of the sea to the river, mother to child, lover to lover.

We are one and the Tao that generates the one unites us eternally objectively universally forever back to where we have always been where we will always be in the middle in the centre in the eternal now no beginning no end forever and ever one.

Acknowledgements

I would like to acknowledge Limerick County Council Arts Office for their generous grant towards the publishing of this book. Special thanks to Joan Mac Kernan, Limerick County Council Arts Officer for her advice and encouragement. I would also like to thank Kerry County Council for publishing an excerpt of the novel under the title of *The Banquet* in Breacadh. Many thanks to Rosemary Canavan former writer in residence for Kerry County Council for her support and direction. I would like to extend my appreciation to my friends in Listowel writers group and the former Scribblers writing group for their help and suggestions.

About the Author; R. M. Hogan

R.M. Hogan has based this first novel *West Dreams East* on experience of teaching in China from 1988 to 1991. During that time she had to be evacuated from the provinces due to the threat of Civil War caused by the Tienanmen Revolution of 1989. Being one of the first evacuees from the provinces she wrote an article for the *Irish Times* on her experience entitled *Isolated in China's Macabre Silence*. She decided to write a novel about the time to protect the identity of those she knows in China and for the creative opportunities afforded by fiction. She is also working on two other novels, one based on her experience of working in the Third World with the UN and another 'coming of age novel' about travelling and working in the USA, entitled *Reviens New Orleans*. She currently works for the V.E.C. Adult Education College in Limerick teaching English to Asylum Seekers.

Part Proceeds of this book will go to the Red Cross for the remarkable work it does in alleviating suffering in this world.